ANDYTOWN
By Frank Fox

This Book is dedicated to all the volunteers' whether from City or Country North or South who fought with bravery and skill and not a little humour. Their story I'm sure is familiar if not the same to all of us involved in the troubles.

CHAPTER 1

I awoke with a start and knocked my alarm clock across the room before it had time to go off with its normal ringing performance, then I was pissed off because I had to jump out of bed and get it from below the locker where it had come to rest .I had been looking forward to this weekend for a couple of months but now that it was here I began to feel a little nervous. It's just that what I was doing this particular weekend was deffo off the Richter Scale in terms of normality, myself and a few buddies, four of us to be exact were going to a Provo training camp in Deepest Darkest Donegal, I had just turned eighteen and me oul Da had given me his spare car a ten year old red VW Beetle that was in great nick and he had insured it and put a year's road tax on it to keep me legal and above board and now I was taking it to an IRA training camp there was a bit of twisted irony in there somewhere.

I got up got washed and dressed and stuffed some Weetabix into me and made sure that I was ready to go before my Ma got up because she would have asked too many questions, she could always tell when I was lying ,my lips were moving and I was always up to no good. As I was closing the door on my way out I shouted into her that i was going away for the weekend and I would see her in a couple of days and as I disappeared out the door I heard her shouting hold you on a minute ya sleekid bastard ye , I want to talk to you, but I was doing a Rhett Butler I was gone with the wind. Seeing as how transport was my responsibility, it was down to me to pick up the lads and get the show on the road. Clinger was my first stop and he was up and ready to go and as excited as me, the second port of call was Jimbo who refused to answer the door and shouted out the window that he had a dose of the flu and his Ma wouldn't let him go and he had a note to that effect. What a wanker, some fuckin terrorist he was, it turned out just a year later he was killed when a bomb he was priming exploded prematurely, killing him. However little did we imagine that lovely summer morning that the grim reaper had buckets of shit and heartbreak in store for all of us. In those days we were forever young and invincible. Next on the list was Twig who was still in bed but was anxious to go, he was always late for everything and a chronic pessimist that would have depressed Coco the clown, Coco was a very unfunny clown with a perpetually painted on face which made him the saddest fuckin clown I had ever seen. Twig fortunately he had a major saving grace in that he told great yarns, super tall tales and the amount of women he claimed to have shagged was beyond belief. Our last port of call was Gilroy's Garage where I filled the tank and then did a runner without paying after all we were on army business. As we motored off on our merry way we picked up Clinger connected up an eight Trak cassette tape to two six volt batteries and we played a load of Rebel music which kept us entertained on our journey. Five hours later we arrived at the Training camp which turned out to be an old run down cottage in the middle of a bog, in the middle of nowhere and not a fuckin sinner to be seen and the door was locked and it started to rain, Oh Joy, it was just typical of the Republican Movement they couldn't organise a piss up in a Brewery.

The windows were the old sash type and we soon had one of them prised open and we were in like Flynn. On the kitchen table covered by a blanket lay an M1 Carbine , a Lee Enfield Mark 4 and a Colt .45 1911 Pistol ,beside them was a big wooden bread bin crammed to the top with ammunition. Our missing hosts had kindly laid out a range just outside off the house with large white rocks marking of the distances in fifty yard increments and split in half three foot long logs as the targets. The next two days we spent firing off thousands of rounds and although nobody turned up to give us any training our shooting skills quickly improved and in the house we found tins of this and that with tea and sugar although unfortunately there was no milk and we were afraid to go looking for a shop in case somebody informed to the local Garda about our presence. After all country people are well known for bring nosey bastards. The IRA standing order at the time regarding a confrontation with the Free State forces was to surrender and under no circumstances to shoot them, well we agreed fuck to that and any unfortunate Garda or Soldier that stumbled upon us would be pushing up the daises in double quick time. The trip back to Belfast was uneventful although we had no idea of the shit storm that awaited us on our return. Apparently the missing Training officers had turned up a few hours after we left and realised we had eaten them out of house and home and used up all of the Donegal Brigade's ammunition. It's as well we took advantage of that weekend as it was all the training we ever got and two days after coming home we were out in action against the British Army.

One of my cousins was a member of Brigade Staff and had organised a night patrol in the Beechmount area just off the Falls road and even though I was relatively young and inexperienced I got to tag along on sufferance. I was given an old Styr rifle a big WW1 weapon with the magazine missing and two rounds of ammunition which had to be breech loaded in order to fire and I was what they called tail end Charlie, not that I gave a shit I was out and actively playing my part in the war. All night long we foot patrolled ourselves around the Broadway area but there wasn't a Brit to be seen and I was getting steadily more pissed off. Eventually it was decided that the five other lads would take a quick recce out on the main falls road and I could stay behind, undercover of a burnt out car and fire a warning shot if anything happened. The plan seemed simple enough to me although I was a bit dubious about being left on my own I crouched down behind the car for a long wait like the new lad in the factory who was told by his boss to go for a long stand. Less than five minutes later I got a fright and the bottom dropped out of my stomach when I heard the crackle of a BA radio right on top of me or so it seemed and my mind started racing as I weighed up my options in a split second, I could fire a warning shot or just break cover and run like fuck and abandon the rest of my patrol who wouldn't know the Brits were behind them. Almost without really thinking I stood up and there not six feet from me stood a British Soldier he was turned away from me and without hesitation I shot him in the middle of the back. Let me tell you John Wayne and the rest of the shilling heroes that never shot a man in the back are fucking arseholes give me sneaky shots all day long and I'll show you somebody with a chance of survival. The crack of the rifle was ridiculously loud and left my ears ringing I can't tell how the BA reacted I was twenty yards away and running as though my life depended on it which in actual fact it did. There was no way the Brits would take any prisoners tonight and I would have to get off the street in the next two minutes before I blundered into other patrols that would be heading for the scene of the shooting. Controlled panic sets in and while most of your brain is in flight mode a tiny part of your consciousness is doing the thinking for you, it's basically a trade in, you have to get off the street asap before you are surrounded but at the same time you have to get at least two streets away to put around one hundred houses in the frame and even though the Brits know your probably in one of them they don't have the manpower to search them all or even twenty percent of them it takes a good hour to raid a house to search every nook and cranny and to P/Check everybody to verify you belong there. They usually only searched the known houses and in the early seventies it was always the houses closest to the scene of the incident that got turned over, as if you would be holed up with a rifle just yards away from where you took the shot. They were as thick as fuck in those days but they were learning. I picked a house and climbed over the yard wall, the back door was on the latch so I went in and locked it behind me, there was an oldish man and woman in the front room and they were sitting having a cup off tea. They sensed something behind them and turned to find me." Jesus Christ "the woman said" what are you doing here". Irish Republican Army I said dont be afraid I just need to stay here until the Brits are gone and it's safe for me to leave. No problem the ould fella said your welcome here and this house is safe it's never been raided. He looked at the weapon I was carrying and said dryly where did you get the rifle son it looks like something from the Somme. Sure enough I did look ridiculous a wee fair haired lad in a school uniform carrying an antique rifle, not the picture that sprang to mind when the TV News gave out the following morning that a young British Soldier had been shot and killed by an IRA sniper the previous night I became sarcastically known to my friends as the Point Blank sniper. I never got much sleep that night because the Brits ran amok all through the area raiding houses and taking some poor unlucky assholes away for interrogation I didn't fancy being in any of their shoes that bright sunny morning. I stayed in the house the whole day as I felt safe there and there was too much security forces activity to risk any of the local IRA coming to pick me up and drawing attention to the safe house although I let the woman of the house go out to the shops and spread the word that I was OK .Later on that night a couple of girls came with a pram and took the weapon away and then one of them came back again and walked me to the main road where I caught a bus up home. This shooting gave me my first kill and made me a minor celebrity among a very small circle of acquaintances it also shoved me into poll position from that time on because killers are hard to come by and once you've proved you have the trick in your head or the elastic conscience that enables you to take a life the IRA will use you again and again until your all used up and you basically can't quit until you're in Prison or dead. I had found that most volunteers in the IRA didn't want to kill they were certainly not cowards but the way we had been brought up gave us religious convictions about Killing, we had to weed these people out because they shot and missed too often and too often things seemed to go wrong , they often didn't know it themselves they wasted operations and got themselves shot because the British Army certainly hadn't got the same unwillingness, they were natural born killers. However you don't see this coming when you set out as a teenager with a head full of republican self-sacrifice and the sum total of your political knowledge is that you are fighting for a United Ireland. The number of people in Andytown that killed on a regular basis was minimal you would be talking about counting on both hands and yet in the early stages of the war in 1970/1971 there were at least 300 to 400 volunteers in the Greater Andytown area. There is really no art to killing any moron can do it but to want to do it you need a special kind of Moron and these are in short supply. It also makes a difference if like the Brits you can be told to believe that the law is on your side and you don't have any legal issues this helps to satisfy your qualms of conscience. Taking a life is one of the worst crimes you can commit and it dosent help when the Cops tell you your committing murder and the IRA tell you that you are a freedom fighter.

CHAPTER 2

I don't want to give the impression here that I was forced to do anything that I didn't want to, I fought because I wanted to and I killed because I was good at it. It was real life Japs and Americans we were the Americans and the Brits were the Japs, we even called them the Japs. Some of the good Japs were bad and some of the bad japs were worse we only came across two in my time that were decent and on two occasions helped to save my life but those stories are for later on.

I have to give the Brits credit where credits due in 1970/1971 they found themselves behind the Eight Ball as far as street fighting was concerned and they lost a lot of men because of the preconceived notion that all working class people thought the same weather they were English or Irish. Assholes like Frank Kitson were hailed as experts in the field of Guerrilla warfare and their ideas were either too extreme for the circumstances in N Ireland or were years out of date. The Brits idea of an IRA operative was of an unemployed denim clad skin head who was as cheeky as he was ignorant. They failed to notice that more attacks took place at the weekend than during the week and that most attacks were in the evening and took place after 5 pm. It doesn't take a genius to work out that a very large percentage of IRA operatives were in gain full employment. The difficulty this raised for us was that we were constantly run off our feet trying to get up early before work time and after work time to enable us to pick good sniping positions which we used mostly in descending order of best ones first. Also when we were too busy chasing women or drinking in the Ex Serviceman's or the PD or any of the watering holes in the West Belfast area we kept the pressure on the Brits and the Peelers by doing what we called Shoot and Scoot.This was a no brainer operation which consisted of three operatives two with semi-automatic rifles and a driver who cruised the local area in a knocked off motor car and looked for targets of opportunity. This was a simple operational format based on the American Drive By Shootings and although it took minimal planning it could be very dangerous and we lost a number of Volunteers this way, probably the most high profile of which were the three Volunteers shot dead on Finaghy Road North who crashed their getaway car up the footpath and accidently killed the Maguire children which in turn gave rise to the Peace People a genuinely reactive circumstance which was taken over by the Brits and used to club the IRA down for their recklessness in shooting in built up areas, in the end the Peace People collapsed and the leaders got the Nobel Peace Prize and a shit load of money by exploiting the tragedy. None the less that was a few years in the future and that sort of collateral damage was difficult to avoid. It is to the credit of all volunteer's in the Irish Republican Army who fought in circumstances in which their enemy was not only mixed up among civilians but as I have since heard British Soldiers admit they actively used civilians as human shields and took cover behind them when conducting P Checks and car and house searches.Im not complaining about this practice the Brits did what they had to do to protect themselves and indeed we were often forced to do something similar. Some people reading this will find it hard to excuse but the average British Squaddie and Provo will readily admit to this if asked but like everything else you had to have been there.

However we spent the rest of the week taking in a new shipment of weapons into Andersonstown and all the members of the 1st Batt were busy distributing them to the other 2 Battalions. I wasn't sorry to see the WW2 weapons go they had served us well but they were old and been through too many hands and they had damaged sights and damp bullets. The new gear was the best and for the first time we felt that our weapons were equal to if not better than the Brits, these were the AR180 Armalite and they were just created by God for CQB in urban warfare. I made sure that we kept the pressure on the security forces and as luck would have it we scored a beauty at the bottom of Finaghy Road North. I was with two of my mates late one evening and we were on a shoot and scoot when we came upon a jackpot two Peelers standing at the junction on the Lisburn road. They were just standing there without a care in the world and I made the decision to hit them up, we drove past them and pulled up about fifty yards away. I got out of the car and was carrying a .357 magnum there was no way you could have taken one of the Rifles they were both Garrands and were too big to conceal. I put the magnum down the back of my trousers and walked confidently towards the Peelers making sure not to make eye contact and to appear as normal as possible you have to seem sort of invisible because people can see stress in your face and their survival instincts go into overdrive. The two of them were total opposites one was about 50 years of age and he looked a bit the worse for wear and the younger one was about 25 years of age and he was as neat as a new pin I judged that he would be the more dangerous of the two so I decided to shoot him first. I slowed down as I reached them gave them a big smile and asked them if they could give me directions to the Ulster Bank, the younger guy smiled back and went to point up the street, I slipped my hand behind my back to get the gun and that's when I realised I had made a mistake . The older cop had never taken his eyes off me and he stepped back and his hand flashed to his holster, I was already committed to shooting the younger cop and had intended on putting two bullets in him but I only had time for one as the older cop had not gone for his gun but realising he wouldn't make it instead lunged at me and I just barely got a bullet into him before he tackled me I steadied myself and finished them off with another bullet each and legged it back to the car and got the fuck out of Dodge.

CHAPTER 3

The Ex-Servicemen's or the Exies as we called it was open and doing a roaring trade so we dumped the gear sent the car to be burned out and headed into have a few pints and chill out. It was against Provo standing orders for volunteers to socialise but we all did it on more than one occasion and it wasn't long before one of the Battalion Officers came over to us and said congratulations its just been on the six o clock news that you hit two off the Black Bastards and they both croaked, now finish your pints and get out of here the Brits will probably raid this place take a few bottles with you and go to a safe house and have a bit of craic.

In the early seventy's the old army formations were still used, Brigades, Battalions and Company's but very soon it became apparent that due to a lack of screening and the need to recruit in large numbers we were adding to the Brits success in breaking down weaker volunteers the level of informers had gone through the roof. This lead to large numbers of weapons being found and the Internment of a significant number of members and consequently morale was at rock bottom. To counter this, the IRA scrapped the Company system and created stand-alone Active Service Units (ASU) which was instrumental in decreasing the volume of informers to a handleable level. Again as I said earlier the Brits were learning all the time. So were we, the father of one of our volunteers was ill and was housebound and he had a radio on which he cold tune in the Brits frequency and we told him of impending operations and he recorded the Brits radio communication during our attacks on them. This meant we could analyse our operations from the second a patrol came under attack and informed their base that they had made contact down to the exact moment they lost track of us. This was when I first came across Zero who at first was one of our most dangerous opponents but as the Brits implemented new counter attack measures his change in technique kept us one step ahead most of the time. Zero was obviously one of a number of British Intelligence Officers that monitored the daily radio chatter and took over when a patrol made contact. Luckily enough for us the squaddies who happened to be under fire at any point in time didn't listen and on more than one occasion told Zero to go fuck himself. For instance we learned from intelligence picked up from a drunken British Officer at a birthday party who was being served by a silver service waitress who happened to have a brother in Long Kesh that the Brits were aware of the fact that we had ran very low on ammunition and that operations were taking place for which volunteers had only two or three rounds in their weapon. You can imagine our shock and horror when a patrol made contact and Zero told the squaddies to run directly at the shooter as he knew that in all likelihood the shooter only had a couple of rounds.Fortunatly for the Brits your average squaddie wasn't that fuckin stupid which left Zero having a conniption as he tried in vain to get them to Kamikaze themselves although they did have some success and a couple of volunteers lost their lives. So also did a few Brits as they played a good thing to long until they discovered that ammunition was back on the menu. A sad fact was that we paid a heavy price for any and all intelligence that we got it kept us ahead of the Posse but I think we always knew that we weren't going to win the game. It was during this period of 71, 72 and 73 that we had the most gear and the trained manpower to take on the Brits in all out warfare. The Yanks being taken to the cleaners by the Vietcong encouraged some of us to push GHQ staff for all out Armageddon but stalling and negativity was all we got from our gallant leaders which made some of us suspicious that there was a mole in the upper ranks maybe more than one and as time later was to prove we were right on and even today I think the full truth has still to emerge mark my words.

Over time our tested and tried system of street fighting began to fail us there were just too many Brits on the street it was either a feast or a famine for hours and sometimes almost a day there wasn't a foot patrol to be seen and then suddenly they came from all the forts at the same time plus small convoys of Ferrets, Seracens and Pigs not to mention the ever present Helicopters. This was when it was most dangerous and lying under cover on a shed roof or in a back garden just didn't cut it we found that it was never the patrol that you fired on that caught or killed you it was the one that you ran into on your Runback. I recall on one occasion I came tearing out from an entry and ran smack into a Patrol and parked on the road in front of me was a Pig and a Jeep. In a split second I realised that to hesitate would mean certain capture or death so I ran firing my M1 Carbine from the hip straight through the middle of them and they were so shocked they just stood there and before they could react I was gone if I'd had time to think about it I never would have done it. As we used to say survival was 80 % skill and 20% luck.

Anyhow we came up with a new Modus Operandi which was surprisingly like our old one except that we took over houses and used them as sniping stations. This required on average two more volunteers depending on who lived in the house and how many people we had to hold hostage. This worked like a charm although we had some memorable monumental fuck ups. On one occasion we took over a house in Lower Atown, I was using an AK 47 and was firing through a back bedroom window into the next street a distance of maybe 100 yards, another volunteer parked a getaway car outside and was watching it and the street from the Livingroom window and two other Volunteers were in the kitchen holding a man his wife and three children hostage. I went upstairs to the back bedroom opened the window and rearranged the beds so that I had a comfortable firing position and settled down to wait. The Brits came up the Glen Road on foot patrol regularly and turned right at the Monagh roundabout and into Fort Monagh so I hoped we wouldn't have long to wait before a target came into view. I was lying relaxed and dozing when I heard the front doorbell ring and the female volunteer went and answered it, there was some conversation and then everything went quiet. Another few minutes passed and there was another ring on the doorbell this went on for another twenty minutes or so until I got totally cheesed off with it and then to cap it all an Irish Jig roared out loudly from downstairs I pulled on my Ballaclava and went down the stairs to see what the fuck was going on. To my amazement the house was full of men, women and children and my two hostage takers were dancing with a load of little girls who were dressed in Irish dancing costumes and seemed to be having a whale of a time. The hilarity stopped however when I stepped into the room carrying the AK and some of the little girls got upset. I called my pal out and asked him what in the name of Jesus was going on. He told me that the family who owned the house were Irish dancing Instructors and they had a competition that morning and the whole Irish dancing lot of them were told to come to that house as they had a bus hired to take them to a competition in Newry. After a quick chat we agreed that we would wait until the bus came and if nothing had happened by then we would call the operation off and call it quits. I went back upstairs and took up my firing position and hoped a target would present itself I hated the thought of all the wasted planning. I was only there a couple of minutes when my mate came up to see me to ask me a favour ,he said the kids had been as good as gold and they wanted to ask if they could have a look at the gun.He said that he had promised them now he didn't want to let them down. I uncocked the rifle and gave it to him and told him that he had 5 minutes but that if he heard me call down he was to get the rifle to me pronto. I went back to watching out for the target again and less than a minute later he was back up to tell me that the kids didn't want him to show them the gun they wanted to see the guy who shoots it. All I could think off was that things were going to shit although I finally agreed but don't ask me why. I was in the middle of being interrogated by the kids who were asking questions a Bishop wouldn't ask you when I got the call from upstairs that we were on, the whole atmosphere changed in a second and the kids got nervous and tense I raced up stairs to my firing position the driver got the car started and the other two blocked the front door lest any of the adults or kids in a panic tried to run out of the house. The foot patrol came up the road right toward me with an RUC man carrying an M1 Carbine in the lead, obviously longing for the safety of the fort. I had the gun cocked and ready to go and I slowly fired 5 single aimed shots at the Peeler who fell to the ground. The distance was only about 75 yards so I felt confident he was fucked.The report of the rifle in the confined space of a house was tremendously loud and as I ran down the stairs and out the door the kids were screaming and some of the adults looked shocked. Less than thirty seconds after the last shot we were heading down the street to the relative safety of the Andytown Road once there we would merge with the traffic and turn down into Stockmans Lane were we had a safe house with a garage to hide both us and the car. At least the runback was uneventful, sometimes things could go totally arseways, your car could fail to start it was easy to flood the engine in a panic and this was the 1970s cars were serviced usually by the owner and on a shoestring budget and you didn't know what sort of piece of junk you were getting hijacked by the volunteers assigned for that purpose. It was much safer to buy a couple of cheap cars and leave them parked up ready for use this saved the added hassle of holding drivers hostage and wandering around the streets armed and searching for a suitable victim of course we often got told to fuck off by the driver, or he sat crying and refusing to let go the steering wheel or he claimed all his relatives were IRA members and he was exempt from hijacking or on occasions a fist fight ensued and the driver got shot in the leg or worse and the whole shebang had to be cancelled and re-scheduled for another time . It was only realised later that putting inexperienced volunteers on hijacking was asking for trouble and we set up squads who unofficially specialised in this. Of course all this sniping was all very well but it somehow didn't scratch the itch for all out mayhem this constant operating under time pressure was necessary for your survival out there but what we really wanted was a chance to stand our ground. It was seriously annoying to hear the Brits constantly claiming the high ground saying we were cowards and wouldn't stand and fight. They really were gobshites and most of them really did believe that crap, when they went out on patrol there were bucket loads of them all backing each other up but when we went out on a job there was no back up for us and we were on our own.

CHAPTER 4:

However there was a situation developing which was to give us the chance to stand our ground. There was a housing problem looming were a lot of catholic families had been made homeless by the protestant pogroms in 1969 and 1970 and these people had never been re-housed. This was creating a crisis in an area of west Belfast called Lenadoon were a lot of protestant families were moving out of their houses leaving them vacant and the Housing Executive wouldn't give the available houses to homeless catholic family's .

There was a march and protest organised for Thursday July 9 1972 during which it was planned by the IRA to forcefully put Catholics into these homes. The IRA and the British Army were on a ceasefire which was in force at the time but it had been decided that if the security forces stopped the protest in Lenadoon Avenue the ceasefire would be broken. The ceasefire had served its purpose anyhow it had given the Provos time to re-group and re-arm. All the local IRA units were called into readiness, weapons and ammunition were handed out and we were told that the signal for the breaking of the ceasefire was that a senior IRA figure who happened to be totally bald would wave his cap in the air and then it was cry havoc and let slip the dogs of war, or as we preferred, it was time to die dog or shite the licence.

My weapon of choice which I had salted away when word of this upcoming firefight had been passed onto us was a Mark 4 Lee Enfield .303 with a set of scopes zeroed for 250 yds.

I had been looking after my little brother until my mother had got back from work and consequently was late for the war and had to run up through the upper Andytown Estate then through to Lenadoon Avenue where I set up shop in a block of flats that looked down the whole avenue. I took my time and watched the Brits down below trying to organise themselves taking cover behind Saracens and Pigs they had pulled across the road. I noticed a small group of three Brits had split off on their own and where setting up a Brit sniper in the porch of a house which looked directly up to our location. The brit was using an L42A1 Marksman rifle and he was taking his sweet time about getting organised, it was obvious he posed more of a threat than the average brit as a lot of our guys were using M1 Carbines and were having to get close to hit their targets. The boyo in the porch was going to do damage if given half a chance and I decided to make sure he didn't get that half chance. I fired a shot at a brit that I could see hiding behind the door of a pig and saw the door jolt obviously a miss but it got my hand in and calmed me down and I turned my attention to the sniper. He was intently scoping out the scene in front of him and from my higher viewpoint I could see one of our lads blasting away with an M1 Garand but he had been spotted and was about to receive the snipers full attention, so I gave the sniper my full attention.

The rifle kicked in my shoulder and when I re -sighted on the sniper he was lying there unmoving and his two buddies had scarpered, he was obviously dead and I was off to a good start. After a while however I found shooting from the elevation of the flats had some serious drawbacks, for those of you who have tried shooting downhill it is very awkward it's a bugger trying to get the holdunder correct and the steeper the hill the more difficult it is. Also you have to raise your head way above the parapet to get the downward angle which on occasion has been known to leave the shooter with a larger cavity in the back of his head where his brains had been. Now I don't have too great an admiration for British Army snipers but I don't believe in making it easy for the bastards so I shifted my position and took another one at ground level among the houses on Lenadoon Avenue. A member of the Official IRA "The Stickies" inquired if he could use my vacated position and I told him to feel free although I hoped he would get one in the noggin. I heard afterwards that he went on to have a very successful few days and he clipped a respectable number of brits so much for my expertise, I was obviously full of shit. I formed up with my own ASU and we ripped it up for over three days, but it catches up with you eventually and I was found by the lads standing with my back to a car with my head propped on the roof and fast asleep in the early morning rain, we were all dropping with tiredness and I decided to take the lads to my house for something to eat and a few hours kip, so we worked our way from Lenadoon into Andytown and slipped into the entry at the side of the house just to get the all clear, the house was supposed to be empty with my family out at school or work but as we were having a well-deserved smoke and a good chat I heard the back door to the alley opening and before you could say O shit, our Alsatian called Mick came barrelling out and straight into the entry. Poor bollox was conditioned to hostility to anyone holding or carrying a rifle and he took a tear at us. I had to shout "Mick stop" three or four times before he gave over the hostility and then he recognised me, he jumped up putting his paws on my chest and licking my balaclava. My Da was slightly enraged to say the least and he said "you may as well come in for a bite to eat and cup of tea" and looked at me as sternly as he could and managed to say in his most irritable accent "I'll be having a word with you later boy" apparently the reason he was home, was my Grandad was a bit under the weather and he had picked him up and brought him to our house for a bit of extra care and attention. My granddad was always an independent old sod and preferred to live on his own. The lads got talking to him and were much impressed, when they discovered he had been in the B.A. and had fought on the Somme, he survived mainly by being a super-potato peeler it wasn't unusual for Irish men to have fought in the B.A. it was a steady job when jobs were scarce. Kept your wee family alive housed and fed during rough days.

He settled down with his cup of tea and proceeded to tell us his story and seeing he was the centre of attention asked my mum for a couple of slices of her freshly baked apple Pie. I thought for a while he was joking when he told us that what saved him from the trenches inWW1 was the fact that he was assigned to the kitchens and there he learned to peel potatoes like a man possessed thereby making himself indispensable to the Cook Sargent. He told me if I was ever in the position of being picked for battle then I was to see the the Cook Quartermaster Sargent and complain that I was the fastest potato peeler in the army and was needed right here in the kitchens otherwise there would be no hot food for the soldiers returning from the front line. It sounded like a load of old spuds to me but you never know sometimes truth is stranger than fiction.

He even told us that my Great Uncle on my mothers side Leading Seaman James Magennis my mother's Uncle was the recipient of the Victoria Cross.It seems on a stormy night in the Straits of Jahore he was the Commander of a mini submarine and was sent out to blow up a Japanese Heavy Cruiser The Takao. The seas were Gale force and his 2 compatriots were sick and unable to complete the mission, when up steps brave Magennis the captain of the Crate to say that he would do it and go to meet his fate. Then he donned his wetsuit and said to every man upon this earth death commeth soon or late and how can man die better than by facing fearful odds for the ashes of his Fathers and the Temples.(That's obviously Horiatis At The Bridge).But he blew the Bastard up and sank it and of course they gave Victoria Crosses to his other companions who were too sick to go. Also because he was a Catholic from Belfast he was excluded from his own Civic reception and wasn't allowed into the city hall to see the Statue that had been erected in his honour. He moved to England sold his VC and died in obscurity. I believe his VC was bought back and is on display somewhere or other.The thing about most Northern Ireland Catholics is they have this dual identity they're brought up on films like The Great Escape,The Guns Of Navarrone,Zulu and The Battle of Britain they identify with your average British Squaddie and would support him against the Germans and the Japs but not the Americans or Argentinians. I remember never missing an episode of Colditz and yet a friend of mine blew up Airiy Neave as he drove into the Commons car park. You can't believe the permeation's of when you would back the Brits and when not. Also most of us have family and friends in England and we work for companies that deal with England, we've been drinking and whoring with them and they are probably the people most like us in the world them and the Scots but Jesus don't get me started on the Scots thats just too mind melting for one book. The important thing is we are closer to fuckin Monkeys than we are to the Orangemen with whom we share our little Island. For them we give no quarter and expect none. The history there is too deep and too raw for there ever to be reconciliation with them and much as we hate them they hate us more. I won't try to recount the number of atrocities that we have visited on one and other during the troubles and generations before but I will tell you this they outscore us more in murderous hatred and pure carnal bile than most civilised nations could countenance. Someday we'll invent a virus called Covid Loyalist , End Game.

It had gotten late and I thought it best if we stayed in a friend of mines flat which was just five houses down from our house so we slipped out of the back door and made our way down , his wife was a nice girl and she insisted on giving us more tea and sandwiches so we lay down on the bed and the floor of the spare room and we were all fast asleep in no time although my friend did sentry for us until about three in the morning when I took it over for the rest of the night. The next morning we all got up and went looking for the Battalion Quarter Master to get some more ammunition and a new rifle or I should say another rifle for Twig so called because he was rail thin and tall. Also I was having problems with my .303 ammunition which was probably WW2 and while some of it was good some of it looked like it had been stored in a river it was damp and rusty and went off with a Boof rather than a Bang. As it turned out the QM when we found him was in a foul humour and told us to fuck off and to put the rounds into some sand and dry them out in the toaster. So we went back to my friends flat and got to work on them, his sister had arrived and she wasn't too bad and Twig started chatting her up she had the biggest cat I've ever seen with her and Twig played a lot of attention to her pussy it lay down in the hearth beside the fire and promptly fell asleep and a couple of hours later when we were nearly finished Twig was still chatting your woman up and loading and unloading his M1 Garand, showing off and generally acting like a school boy , I told him to stop the messing and get ready to rock and roll but he just had to have on last go at acting the ejit and he knelt down beside the fire and un cocked his weapon letting a round fly out of the Breech his intention was to catch it in his hand an unnecessary thing to do however he missed the round and it flew into the fire which was blazing hot and settled down in the red hot coals I stuck my hand into the fire and tried to flick it out but it went in deeper Twig tried to grab it and burned his hand and it went in deeper I grabbed the fire tongs and tried to get it but it went in deeper still. I shouted Take Cover and everybody in the room dived for the door to the kitchen we were laying like a pile of bodies when the cartridge went off with a Bang and a big screeching fur ball flew past me and out the window never to be seen again there were flaming bits of coal burning holes in the oilcloth all around the living room I told my mate we would pay to get it re-laid and decided to leave as I reckoned we had out stayed our welcome . A volunteer with a car came and picked us up and drove us up to Lenadoon on the way he briefed us informing us that the Brits had moved hundreds of more troops into the fight and we needed to be extra careful. I thought about it and decided that we would go by way of Stewartstown Avenue and down Mizzen Gardens which would flank the Brits and hopefully they wouldn't see this coming. With the hundreds of other soldiers and the fact that we had been informed that other areas of Belfast had erupted into Gun Battles and that we would have one last rattle and call it a day.

CHAPTER 5:

On the way up Stewartstown Avenue we split into two's and made our way around and into Mizzen Gardens. I had told the lads to hold their fire so as not to give our position away. The Brits were like a hoard of busy little bees out in Lenadoon Avenue and they were using Snipers with spotters and our lads were still giving it their all but they were about to be seriously outclassed. It was just then that I saw four volunteers about to get trapped and cut down, there were three armoured vehicles moving into position to cut them off and leave them without cover and with their backs to the field alongside Lenadoon Avenue once they were flushed out they would be easy pickings and the Brit snipers would take them out

There was Brit who seemed to be in charge of the little convoy it was impossible to tell his rank from the distance between us not that it mattered anyway, he had to be stopped as he was the only one in the convoy who seemed to know what he was doing. They had their backs to us and couldn't have been set up better if they'd been in a shooting gallery. I signalled to the lads that I was going to take the one standing up on the back of the Pig and they each took a different target I fired first and I could see through my sights him getting thrown like a rag doll to the road I picked another couple of targets and was pretty sure that I had at least wounded them, one of the other lads got a hit as well and I waved them in and we retreated back the way we had come. It had been a very successful days' work and I didn't want to spoil our success by taking unnecessary casualties this late in the game. A celebration was called for but we had one in a call house rather than risk being scooped drinking in one of the Clubs or

Pubs about the area.

It was a great night and we sang rebel songs and re –counted our deeds of daring do and exaggerated our kills and wounding until we had defeated the whole British Army more importantly than any of this I nearly got the knickers off a Cumin na Man girl and all in all we felt pretty good about ourselves it was a night to remember because we didn't get too many of them and as they say make hay while the sun shines. I had been blessed that all of this was occurring during the school holidays so I wasn't under any time pressure and anyway I had done well in my O' Level exams and was expecting to go back to school and take my A 'Level exams before going on to University to get a Degree in something or other that would enable me to get a good job in the future. Sadly this wasn't to be as I was informed by my dad that I wasn't going back to school as he was of the opinion that I would be wasting my time as the only future he could see for me was the inside of a Gaol cell or a pine box. He told me as far as he was concerned people in the IRA didn't have a future but that he would pull some strings with a friend of his and get me a job as a Clerk in an Import/Export Company. To say I was devastated was an understatement and I sulked and argued but to no avail my Da was not the type to change his mind when he had made it up, he was a man who would not suffer fools gladly. He supported the Republican movement and would like to have seen a United Ireland but more importantly he had a wee family to rear and had to keep working to keep us fed and a roof over our heads. Like most of the men of his generation in Northern Ireland he considered himself lucky to have a job and worked for Belfast Corporation Transport (City Bus) until he retired at age 65.He kept to himself was a staunch friend and never had a bad word to say about anyone his greatest love was the ITGWU and he was the shop steward for the Buses for most of his life. His best friend was a Protestant who was his conductor when he was a driver before he rose to the dizzy heights of Inspector. This man Victor was his name used to come over to our house on his day off and cut myself and my brother's hair, and on occasion when our neighbours spotted a good thing he would cut the hair of half the street. Of course this was just before the Troubles he never came after that but him and my Da remained good friends up to the day Victor died.

I quickly found that this work business was wreaking havoc with my freedom fighter lifestyle and I found it particularly galling to seeing the security forces walking around our area unchallenged. It was also extremely difficult to fit in the type of free flowing gun attacks which used to be our bread and butter and which we found so successful, so I called a meeting of our ASU and we decided to change tactics, out went the shoot and scoot and the hijacking of cars and the on the street firefights and in came the use of our intelligence volunteers. They hadn't been of much value through no fault of their own it was just our free flowing operations system didn't need much planning but they promised to deliver the goods and when they did they really did. One of the first gems to come our way was a judge who dropped his daughters off at a girls convent school on the Falls Road, he did this almost every morning and he also gave us the added bonus that he did this early in the morning which gave me a chance to nut him and still get to work on time. This was the first time in the present troubles that a member of the Judiciary was to be targeted and we knew there would be uproar and the RUC would be out to find the villains responsible. Good luck to them. This one hit would be worth fifty dead brits because the establishment doesn't like to be targeted. The Intelligence squad were more than helpful we had decided that we needed a motorbike to do this job and much to my amazement they just happened to have the very thing which they had confiscated from some hoods about three weeks previous and had parked in a garage just for an occasion such as this. Neither myself nor any of the rest of the ASU had ever ridden a motorcycle and we had to look for someone who fitted the bill for this operation. I was going as pillion passenger and I didn't like working with strangers who might panic if things went wrong or even if things didn't go wrong, also this wasn't a big job to carry out but the ramifications afterward were going to cause a shit storm. The Special Branch would pull in every informant, tout and general asshole they could lay their hands on and shake the trees very vigorously and keep shaking them in the hopes that something would fall out, so although this wasn't technically a difficult operation it was a bad one to cut your teeth on. I needn't have worried First Battalion staff cane up with an extremely experienced driver for the motor bike who was from the East Tyrone Brigade of the Provo's and who could drive anything with wheels. So the following week the two of us pulled up alongside the target and when he had let his daughters and friends out of the car I climbed off the motorbike and walked to the driver's side window and shot him 5 times in the head and chest with a Browning Pistol. Up to this point what you're doing doesn't seem real it's only when the screaming starts and the bystanders around you are frozen into hunched shapes and clutching one and other for the illusory protection that being a fellow victim gives you but in my experience the hi pitched screaming brought on by terrible terror and loss would tear at your soul if you had one. There is something final and sad about killing on a grey damp and overcast day it makes you feel that you're already a mourner at a long, long funeral.

While all this was going on the Brits and the RUC were continuously nibbling away at our manpower mostly interning and killing our volunteers in a war of attrition. It was hardly noticeable at first but then you began to notice faces missing and the answer to where's such and such was always nearly the same, oh he got lifted last week and sent to the Kesh. We didn't realise it then but our good days were bad and our bad days were worse. However there was always light at the end of the tunnel and for me that was new weapons to fuck around with we had gotten a shipment of AR180 Armalities which had more than levelled the playing field as far as shoulder fired weapons were concerned and even placed us slightly ahead of the SLR. In time we got all the Middle East gear from Gadhafi and Eastern Bloc hand we were awash with FN 's ,G3 's H&K's and AK47's to mention but a few despite all this I still had a fond feeling for the oul Aramlite , it was a man stopper it was accurate up to 100 yds (that's far enough for CQB) and with the Butt folded down it could easily be shoved up an anorak or jacket and was easy to conceal after a job. It's just Murphy's Law that when we finally got this bounty of small arms we hadn't got the people to properly exploit it. It so happened that along with the Armalites came some unexpected extras in the form of Mortars and Grenades all brand new and in pristine condition also as we were never going to get replacement Mortar Bombs the tubes were then disposable like the grenades they were a one shot deal. All the ASU's from Belfast to the border we queuing up to get them but our QM was well respected and managed to get us six Mortars with 12 Bombs and a box of 8 grenades to be honest most of this gear went to the towns and Cities as they were the only places you could get close enough to the Brits to use them.

CHAPTER 6:

It was decided that we would use the mortars first since they were the most awkward and we needed 4 men to do the job that's 2 teams of 2 to fire 12 bombs out of 6 tubes this was the minimum people we could get away with and be able to fire all the bombs still leaving us time to escape we were firing from the back gardens of one street and over a row of houses and we were taking no firearms with us so we were running clean through the street behind us and laying up in two houses we had arranged and were the occupants were not known republicans but could be trusted. Silver City was the Fort we chose and Sunday was the best day for the attack because the Brits usually had a lay in on a Sunday like the rest of the world and as no patrols would be out it would maximise the casualty's and as an added bonus it would help ensure that our runback was clear.

A van dropped us off and we off loaded the mortars and as we were setting them up which only took a matter of minutes the van pulled away and we were on our own. There was no use in hanging about so we fired the first 2 mortars simultaneously and we were expecting a massive explosion but instead got a loud Poynng we had the next 2 in the air before the first 2 hit their targets and at least they made a satisfying Whump when they went off. The next one we fired was a dud but the next 5 went off like Vesuvius, well not really but they weren't too bad either. Ambulances came and went for hours afterward and we could hear the sound off heavy diggers working away although we couldn't have seen anything as the walls of the fort were around 30 feet high. Our runback was uneventful but we were stuck in Inishmore Crescent for the whole day as the Brits ran amok especially when they found the empty mortar tubes in the back gardens of Glasmullen Gardens. Its nerve wracking sitting in somebody's house praying it won't get raided, at least this time we hadn't got any weapons in the houses with us. It still all depends on what sort of manpower the Brits had available on the day in question as it takes about 2 hours to raid a house and there is about 60 houses on average on a street to put it in mathematical terms it takes a shit load of Brits to raid just one street and still have the men available to put out patrols the next day. Then it's soul destroying to watch the 6.00pm news that night and find that your operation doesn't get a mention and the Brits are not acknowledging that any such event took place. It didn't surprise us though as even if a number of Brits had been killed or injured this would be easily outweighed by the fact that the British Government would not want the great unwashed to know that the IRA were wacking them out of it with mortar bombs and there was a possibility the IRA weren't the incompetent half assed Gobshites as portrayed by the media. The media were mouthpieces for the establishment and they lambasted us on any opportunity so we were relatively careful not to give them the opportunity, which I nearly did less than a week later. Myself and a volunteer called Clinger were driving up the Andersonstown Road when we passed by a lone foot patrol P Checking people coming out of mass in St Agnes Chapel, we were transporting an Armalite Rifle up to lower Andytown and not to look a gift horse in the mouth we decided to do a shoot and scoot. Clinger wheeled right at the Busy bee and down ST Agnes Drive to the back gate of St Agnes Chapel we saw no Brits anywhere around so I jumped out with the rifle and ran down the steps at the side of the Chapple. I hadn't even got face cover but the side of the chapel was deserted and anyway I was committed at this stage, I cocked the rifle and took a peek from the side of the wall onto the main road the Brits were still there and had some guy up against a wall searching him. I took cover drew a deep breath raised the rifle and went to step into the clear to get a couple of shots off when I was grabbed by the neck from behind by the Parish Priest.Well fuck me sideways I was dumbfounded I rammed him against the Chapel wall and he let go my neck but immediately grabbed the muzzle of the gun with both hands and tried to wrench it the out of my hands but I was holding onto the butt and forearm stock and I began to ram the muzzle into his chest all this time I had the safety off and my finger on the trigger. I told him to Fuckin let go the gun but he pulled all the harder, let go you crazy bastard I hissed at him very aware that the Brits were only 10 yards away around the corner of the chapel he called me a sinner and an evil man and a murderer and anything else he could think off. If the Brits had only looked around the corner the two of us were fucked. I made up my mind to shoot him as he had left me with no choice but with a last fling of the dice I gave him a boot in the balls which did the trick and he let go, he was rolling on the ground and to my utter shock called me a Cunt. Well I thought that I'd heard everything the Parish Priest called me a cunt. I ran back up the side of the chapel and as I jumped into the car beside Clinger I was roaring with laughter and just waved him to go as I couldn't talk. I heard that he gave out about us the following day at Mass and said that we had tried to kill him, he forgot to mention the fact that he had tried to take the gun off me and nearly got me caught or worse. An always an anyways I decided to put the bold Parish Priest behind me and get on with business. My job was causing me hassle due in no small part to the fact that I was regularly late and I was told that if I continued on with this behaviour I would get a warning so I decided to act the good employee for a few weeks until things had blown over in actual fact the whole ASU needed a break as every one of us was mentally exhausted. It was during this two week layoff that I had one of the nastiest experiences of my life one that even today I don't like to recall too often. One Friday night I was making my way home after a night out on the booze although I hadn't had too much to drink maybe six or seven pints over the course of the whole afternoon and night. I usually walked home through the Andersonstown estate so that if I came across a Brit foot patrol and got P Checked and arrested there was usually somebody walking by that you could call out your name to and ask them to tell your family that you'd been lifted also it was easier to avoid Brits in the estates as people warned passers-by that there was a foot patrol in such and such a street and you could always take an alternate route. On this night for some reason probably because I was coming from the Glenowen Pub I decided to come straight up the Glen Road which had no street lighting and at that time was lined along one side with very large pine trees and along the other with Church housing big convents that stood way back off the road behind eight foot walls with locked gates. I was striding along trying to look as innocent as you please, just an ordinary dude sauntering home from a night on the town. Then I heard the jeeps coming up the road behind me and I put my head down and tried not to look at them or make eye contact it was two open back jeeps full off Brits and they pulled in right beside me and roared at me to stop. Three or four of them surrounded me and one of them patted me down to see if I was carrying a fire arm which I wasn't but they always lived in hope that they would catch some poor bugger armed so they could at beat the shite out of him or best option croak him. The radio operator asked me my details and called them into base which in their case was Fort Monagh a fuckin hell hole if ever there was one and my heart skipped a beat when I heard the call back from the fort " Fresh Meat" this meant you were to be lifted and brought to the fort for interrogation . Initally they were going to call a Pig and that would have been SOP only I heard the base call for me to be brought in by the Jeep patrol. The brits squeezed up in one of the jeeps and told me to hop in like they were giving me a lift somewhere instead of arresting me and taking me in for their buddies to beat on me. One of the brits complained about the tight squeeze and the patrol commander offered to let him wait there until the jeeps got back " No fucking thanks " he said and the other Brits began to hoot and catcall to him . The convoy took off and did a quick about turn and set off back the way they had come and in less than five minutes I was being driven in through the gates of the Fort. Two Brits came out of the interrogation block and told the jeep patrol to take me around back and they would be met by somebody that would take me off their hands, there was an uncomfortable silence in the jeeps and the Brits around me suddenly didn't want to look me in the face

We drove around back and into a small compound where there were two Brits in plain clothes waiting on me they told me to hop out sharpish and walked me straight through a swing door and into what looked like a briefing room there was a chair at the front of the room in front of a blanket covered table and there were eight chairs on the other side of the table. The brits then told me to take the top seat and to sit down and make myself comfortable and they sat down facing me and stared in silence at me for around ten minutes. They never did any of the usual stuff they had on the couple of previous times I had been in for interrogation, like taking my watch, emptying my pockets, taking my details and fingerprinting me. If I had ever been a bit tipsy I certainly wasn't now, I was wide awake. One of the Goons dragged me off the chair and forced me back against the wall by tripping me little did he know I was a 2nd Black Belt in Judo but you don't fight back in a situation like that its best to let them have their power trip rather than risk serious damage or worse from his buddies. While this was happening the other Goon turned his back toward me and from what I could see he cleared his Browning, I knew what was coming next, he grabbed me by the throat and shoved the muzzle of the gun into my mouth. The other Goon then told me if I didn't give the names and addresses of two IRA men in the next minute he would pull the trigger and they would dump me out the road and blame it on the UVF. The only thing you can do at a time like this is get angry, I mean don't give a fuck angry so angry that you don't care for your personal safety anymore and start shoving them back , anyway I was getting a real bad vibe from the way this scenario was going and they knew it. As if on que in trooped six other munchkins who sat on the seats facing me then the other two sat down and the whole eight of them stared directly into my eyes in dead silence for about ten minutes. They were all dressed in what you could call Army civvies , runners, jeans or slacks and crew cuts they all looked young and one or two of them looked a bit self-conscious at this carry on. Suddenly one of my two integrators jumped to his feet knocking his chair over and began to give me the slow hand clap the other seven followed suit. In my opinion the term surreal is used to often but it really suited this farce I decided the only answer to this was to act totally unafraid and be cool, so with a titanic effort I turned the anger in my face to amusement sat down in my chair put my hands under my chin and started to laugh. The clapping slowly faded away and in the silence that followed I said "I don't know who writes your script but you want to get somebody better" the two interrogators had faces looked like thunder obviously their little psychological warfare show meant to impress their handpicked audience had been torpedoed and I knew there was going to be a price to be paid by me.The two main men closed up the show and then brought in three new guys to see me these three were dressed in combats with no jackets only a tee shirt. One of the interrogators stepped close to me and looked me in the eye and said "Just one thing have you ever killed anybody if you have you don't have to say anything just blink, just blink that's all " he stared at me intently and suddenly jerked his head toward me and I blinked and he smiled and said "That's OK you can go now".

They all disappeared this time and I was left on my own, I looked around the interrogation room without seeming to obvious about it and there was nothing to be seen I then opened the drawer on the desk that was sitting in front of me and to add to my worries there was a .38 Smith and Wesson revolver in the desk drawer. Was this a set up or what, like I was supposed to believe that someone had been careless enough to have left this weapon just lying around no shagging way I closed the drawer and let on that I hadn't seen it . About twenty minutes later

I heard someone coming down the corridor and in stepped an enormous brit with sergeant's stripes on, he looked like Windsor Davies in It Aint Half Hot Mum and he gripped me by the arm and said "you're coming with me, you're getting released". He walked me out and into a compound that I didn't recognise and from there into the main compound that I was used to seeing from my odd visits for interrogation. There wasn't a sinner in the whole compound it seemed like the fort had been deserted and the only two living people left were the sergeant and I. As we approached the main gates I started to pull back and the Brit stopped for a second said to me out off the corner of his mouth "Look son I don't like what's going on here I'm giving you a heads up, when you get outside these gates run for your life and don't stop for anything" and then everything happened at once. He opened the gate and shoved me out and the first thing I saw was a white saloon car rolling along Monagh road almost level with the dirt track lane up to the fort. There was one guy steering the car and two guys pushing as if the car had cut out. One of them looked up from pushing the car saw me and shouted in a broad Belfast accent " "hey fella give us a push will ya".Well I tell you I ran like my feet had wings down across the hard core away from the dirt track and across Monagh Roundabout. One of the guys ran after me shouting" don't run we only want a push" and then I heard two shots, there was a six foot wire fence along the footpath that ran around the roundabout and I cleared it like Dick Fosbury I don't think they came after me though it wouldn't have mattered anyway I was up side entries' over coal sheds and across streets I knew to a call house not two hundred yards away were I got a Beretta 9 mm and I was in such a temper that I ran back the way I had come looking to kill the fuckers.

CHAPTER 7:

It was some months later that I realised that I had, had my first but not my last run in with the MRF a section of the British Army who's brief was to kill Catholics and IRA members if they could get them and to recruit IRA informer's and double agents into the MRF and encourage them to murder innocent Catholics and blame it on Loyalist Paramilitaries. Eventually we ran them to ground and executed two just from Andersonstown alone, Vinty Heaherington and Myles Mc Grogan and routed the rest of the bastards whose names we have locked away, they may never come back. However if I have time I'll come back to this and speak more about these cowardly animals who backed up by the British Army were encouraged to run the streets committing murder with no risk to themselves.

The end result of this was that I felt too wound up to enjoy my remaining down time and as my time was spoiled I decided to do likewise to the lads, as it turned out we were all fed up with the inactivity, we were like adrenalin junkies and our fix was killing and risking our lives. There is nothing like the rush you experience when you've just escaped death by the skin of your teeth this applies to almost everybody and anybody who has just had a lucky escape and can't help but laugh about it. So I wasn't surprised when I found the lads ready and rearing to go. I decided that we may as well use the Grenades we had stored away before Battalion took them off us, I had thrown assorted Nail bombs and I found them not much use in a combat situation they were too heavy and there was too much footering about trying to get them lit especially in damp weather. The grenades we had were top of the range blowieups we called them

Japanese Light Eggs obviously they were little and the fly away lever had two slanty little circles on either side of it, just kidding they were little smooth drab olive green and packed full of ball bearings cute but lethal. Again as with the mortars we didn't need any weapons and as when the grenades exploded there would be fuck all left to leave any clues and as we had nothing incriminating on us on our run back. All we had to do now was to find a spot for the ambush that would get us in close to the Brits, protect us from the explosion and put none of the local population at risk not an easy task. I spent days trying to get somewhere and was just a bout to give up when Clinger of all people came up with a beauty. It was the side garden of a house facing Holy Child Primary School and the wall around the garden was roughly eight feet high. Clinger had watched it for a few nights and it seemed that a Brit foot patrol often stopped there with the wall at their back and called into base and took five to have a piss and a smoke. There was no use in sussing the place out again as Clinger had already done a good job and anyway you can overly complicate a nice simple little job like this to the point that the Brits begin to smell a rat and its then that you can get yourself ambushed by looking for belt and braces when you would be better off just going for it. We had to collect the grenades and I found they were in an arms dump in a house in Edenmore Gardens occupied by an elderly man and his Down's syndrome son. Arms dumps like this are ideal as the occupants can be trusted and who would expect that a house like this held a veritable arsenal of weapons and explosives, to the best of my knowledge that house was never and has never been raided. The owner was a nice oul skin and he insisted on making us a cup of tea while his son George finished off polishing up the grenades as some smart arse had told him that grenades worked better with a rub of Brasso, we got out of there fairly sharp although I never bothered complaining to The Batt Q.M. who was a dick and wouldn't have cared less had wee George painted the bloody things Green White and Orange.

There was a lot of narking going on about this operation as some bucket mouth had spilled the beans to Na Fianna Eireann who were sort of the junior wing of the IRA and some of their longer serving members were trying to muscle in on the job. I couldn't really blame them they did a hell of a job for us acting as scouts on a lot of operations, carrying weapons from place to place, hijacking cars and generally risking their freedom and their lives doing all the thankless tasks that the IRA didn't have time for. They ranged in age between fourteen and eighteen and their purpose was to learn about field craft and weapons so that they would be ready to replace lost volunteers when the need arose. The fact was the need didn't arise that often, on the contrary we were losing men at a steady rate but that we hardly ever replaced them from the ranks of the Fianna because by the time they were needed they were too well known to the Brits they were all used up and two minutes in Silver City or Fort Monagh had them telling everything they knew from the Easter Rising to infinity and beyond. They lived on the promise from us that we would give them a chance on a job now and again and if they did well we would move them into full time IRA. This wasn't always regularly possible as they had little firearms experience and were mostly too young. This was why this particular operation had caught their fancy they knew there were no firearms involved and all was required was to lob a couple of hand grenades over a wall and scarper. I wouldn't talk to them myself as they weren't allowed to deal directly with the ASU but I sent them instructions that they were to stand down over this and they promptly sent back word for me to" fuck off", there was virtually mutiny in the ranks and they stopped co-operating and disappeared into the estate where we couldn't find them. Eventually we gave in and told them that we would use two of them on the job and it was arranged for the following night. Our runback was between North Green from where we would throw the grenades to a safe house in Corby Way that was all set to take the three of us myself and the two Fianna boys we would each lob two grenades. It was a cloudy night and it seemed like a long time waiting for the Brits to come, so long in fact that I was almost about to call it off, there would always be another night and then a knock at the window let us know that the Brits had arrived and it was time to go . We sneaked along the back gardens and I was startled to see two extra bodies in our crew I whispered my anger to them all but it was too late to turn back by then, the little bastards had snookered me rightly and had brought along another three Fianna so now apparently we were going to throw one grenade each" well another one for the pot as my Da used say. I went last after each of the lads had dropped his grenade over the wall the brits only had time to hear the soft thuds as the first two hit the ground on their side of the wall and then there was an unmerciful double explosion and we were all instantly deaf to be honest there was no hesitation from the lads each one played his part and long after I had dropped my grenade the screams of the wounded could be heard streets away.

All the next day we had to stay in the safe house in Corby Way as the Brits had the whole area sealed off and were methodically going house to house unfortunately for them they were in North Green the street were the attack had taken place and not the adjoining street were we were holed up . Still two of the Fianna although they had done a stalwart job the previous evening showed a bit of nervousness and nearly shit themselves when the paper boy came hammering on the door for his money. I had decided to wait until the coast was completely clear before I let people filter out of the house for two reasons, the first was that the Brits may have a kill squad or squads hidden in the neighbouring streets in the hope that somebody would break cover and give away our safe house or simply one of the Fianna would get scooped up and end up in Fort Monagh and squeal on the rest of us in the safe house and us with not a weapon between us. It was usually Fort Monagh because they handled most off the interrogations and had the facility's for them if breezeblock walls and bare rooms could be termed facility's and in the coming years I spent a lot of time there getting my arse kicked and as I said earlier once nearly murdered in that place. Any way the Brits huffed and puffed and found fuck all and eventually after they had handed out enough kicking's to the local population they shagged off back to their lair. It was only later that we found out that most of the BA foot patrol caught in the Grenade ambush had lost mainly feet and lower limbs and as we say God is Good they all played for the Regimental football team.

CHAPTER 8:

It was just one of those times that you decide to take your foot of the accelerator and your finger off the trigger and just sit back and chill when you can always depend on the Orangemen to throw a spanner in the works. This particular spanner belonged to a loyalist murder gang operating out of the Kells Avenue Estate and situated right facing The Woodburn Army Camp. They were just in the middle of Catholic West Belfast and were using their location to kidnap and kill unsuspecting and innocent Catholics who had to go through the junction of Blacks Road, Kells Ave and Suffolk Road to get home at night usually some poor sod on his own with a couple of drinks taken. As the area all around there was part of Andytown it was left up to us to make them think twice before they did it again. At first we did a couple of drive bye's which left one man dead and another one injured but this failed to register with them and I decided to ramp things up a notch. This makes me sound as though I was somebody with a senior rank and the right to make and implement policy decisions like the one I was about to make but the case was , I was only the equivalent of an ASU OC but one who all the volunteers knew and would obey my instructions without feeling the need to question them. I had just been informed that the 1st Batt QM had been lifted by the Brits and had gone for his tea to Long Kesh and I was told along with others to collect up move and re- dump all our weapons and explosives and while doing this I discovered something interesting we had 5 mortar tubes and 15 bombs still available so I promptly took charge of them to hold for a rainy day and I was sure one would come along pretty soon.

There were some Gobshites in the IRA who thought it was a Corporate Organisation and they revelled in getting promotions, to Battalion ,Brigade and GHQ staff what they didn't realise was that they were only message boys with a title, the real movers and shakers of the IRA were household names and they ruled through a hierarchy of old Staunch republican families whose fathers had been out in the forty's and fifties campaigns and who's Grandfathers had had taken part in the Easter Rising and the war of independence which followed. Also it was a good excuse not to take part in operational activities you know the old saying give a man a bowler hat. They were also the assholes who had to have a company of Fianna boys and army women to help them move a gun from here to there, like it was a big deal and for all this pricking about they still ended up in Long Kesh because they still trusted the Fianna who as I said before couldn't hold their water. The rest of us in the ASU, s didn't bother with this secret squirrel stuff we just carried any weapons we needed for operations or personal protection cocked and loaded and we were ready willing and able to come out blasting should the need arise. It was in view of this arseways command structure that I was able to put my plan for mayhem on the Kells Ave Estate into operation. I got in touch with our IO who was our ASU liaison with Batt Staff and told him sort of vaguely that we were going to give The Kells Ave Est a rattle at the weekend preferably Sunday come dinner time. This was obviously a gross missundestatement , as what we had planned was to fire the 15 mortars into the Estate and then drive in five vans eight men to a van each with the address of local and well known Loyalist Paramilitary leaders and go straight into their houses after them and to also kill whatever men they came across in the houses or walking around the area. It was a nice straightforward plan and for the rest of the week we lifted the dumps that we had helped to move previously that month. It was also very handy that the ASU, s didn't communicate with each other and it never dawned on anyone the scale of the operation we were undertaking, the security system that worked against the Brits also worked against our own side. It was impossible to keep track of the shenanigan's going down at this time mainly because in 1972 there were around 11,000 shootings and over 2,000 bombings and even though our job was on a grand scale to us it was really not much bigger than one of the border Units attacking an RUC station. At least that was the tongue in cheek excuse that we were going to give the GHQ Staff after it was all over and the shit had proverbially hit the fan, we reckoned on losses of 2 to 3 men but we believed that we would kill upwards of 100 loyalist paramilitaries and general protestants who would make up collateral damage. This was a lesson learned from watching the Vietnam War and how the Viet Cong had won against the Americans. After all was this a fuckin war or wasn't it and were we really trying to win or just wear the Brits down in a war of attrition. For the first time in our history we had the man power the weapons the willingness to go the extra mile and the confidence in ourselves that a United Ireland was achievable in our lifetime.

I went to sleep on Saturday night in a spare bedroom in one of our call houses or should I say I tried to sleep but it was hard to come by. The amount of things that could go wrong worried me, something always goes wrong it's a fact well known to people who manage men in stressful situations that someone always decides they have a better way of doing something and it never occurs to them that there can often be a knock on effect that they don't see. Or it can simply be that they don't want to take part in what's about to happen and they go out of their way often subconsciously to do something to scupper the show. As I lay there I realised that I had done the best job I could in setting this up and all the worrying in the world would not do any good so I settled down to get a few zzzzz when I thought of something else, I knew in my heart and soul that I had overstepped the bounds of my authority and there was going to be hell to pay I wasn't worried about the amount of casualty's that were going to be sustained if this operation went to plan I didn't give a rats ass about death and destruction I've always had a sneaking suspicion that I'm a sociopath with psychopathic tendencies or vice versa I'm not sure if it makes any difference. My main worry was that I would end up in a shallow grave in the Wicklow Mountains were the IRA gets rid of unwanted problems. I then reconciled my body to science and my soul to Walt Disney and finally got some sleep. Sunday morning finally arrived and I arose refreshed and starving as I had very little to eat the previous day because I was so busy I had forgotten to get anything. The woman of the house seemed to sense that I was hungry and fed me up with a big fry, for which I was extremely grateful after that I felt a lot better and as I looked outside on a new day I believed all was possible and all a body had to do to change it was to get out there and make it happen. As it turned out making it happen was absurdly easy the most difficult problem we had was getting all the vans, but one of our lads came up trumps and we became the proud possessors of a small fleet of Transit Vans belonged to a Building company which was closed on a Sunday and had an old watchman who looked after the plant when it was closed and had the keys to all the equipment hanging conveniently in a wall box in his little Portakabin. We considered killing him but he had been cheerful and co-operative and was a catholic so we tied him securely took his driving licence gave him a half bottle of whiskey which he could just manage to get to his mouth by tilting his head and supping the whiskey from the bottle tried to a piece of string hanging from a shelf above his head. Now I wouldn't go so far as to say he was as happy as a pig in shite but once he realised he wasn't going to be killed and there was free Gargle he promised us that he would play his part like a true gentleman, scholar and Saturday Night Republican so we told him we were the IRA and if he did anything stupid we would come for him and his family. So we took one of the vans out and picked up the mortars and bombs got in touch with the rest of the men and told them that we would use the Building Company as our jumping off place. I sent another van on a run to a couple of dumps to pick up the weapons which were more than satisfactory being a mixture of Armalites , SKS, M1 Carabine's , and a half dozen Luger Pistol to be on the safe side. All the arrangements had been made and the Go signal was the mortars exploding in the estate but sadly it never got to that. Just two minutes before the kick off a few men were seen approaching us and even from a distance I could see at least two of them were Brigade Staff Officers and I knew the game was up. I was told in no uncertain terms to stand down the operation as it wasn't sanctioned and that I was ordered to report to a Brigade meeting house the following Saturday. They then turned and walked away in the knowledge that no matter how badly miffed we were feeling that their orders would be obeyed to the letter.

As it turned out I never had to answer for my indiscretion as on the following Friday which was 21/July, I was involved in an operation which later became known as Bloody Friday and all notions of me reporting to Brigade Staff for Courts Martial were scrapped, in Lyndon Johnson famous words about J Edgar Hoover they would rather have me inside the tent pissing out than outside the tent pissing in. They did however banish me to fight in upper A 'town with very little support as most of their volunteers had been Interned leaving only a handful of Female Army volunteers to keep the flag flying, but I soon found that they were fearless and the equal of any man I had fought with and what they lacked in firearms skill or physicality they more than made up in Intelligence and Innovation and the willingness to give anything a shot. The reverberations of Bloody Friday rumbled on and on and I thought the most sensible course of action at the time was to just keep my head down and ride out the storm of public indignation. Anyway I was having trouble in work, not because of the work itself which was fairly easy and wasn't exactly mentally taxing it was all straight forward administration and filing. The problem lay in that no matter how much I tried not to, I was taking too many days leave both sickness and holiday days. A comrade of mine had heard indirectly that I always seemed to be off when things were happening and given the fact that I worked for a mixed Catholic and Protestant employer it thought it was doubly important to keep my head down at this particular time. I decided two things then, firstly I decided to apply for promotion in my job which involved taking some internal administrative exams and I hoped that this would fool my employer into thinking that I was really Goody Two Shoes and make it seem that any suspicions they had were unfounded. Secondly I decided that I would play the white man and I would get the women army volunteers together and see what sort of loosely structured active service unit I could make up. Also I had to get to know them as I had virtually no interaction with any of them at all and didn't even know their names although there were one or two who's names I recognised because I knew their brothers, who were in Long Kesh, were else. I wasn't celibate of course but I just didn't have the time for taking on a girlfriend they were just not worth all the hassle that you had to put in just to get a ride and any way I had just recently had an extremely unpleasant encounter that soured me on women for a while to come yet. On top of everything else I had gone to an all-male primary school and an all-male secondary school and I had very little experience of the fairer sex and couldn't have chatted one up for a bet.

Although about a month ago I was out with the lads and we decided to do a pub crawl of the Falls Road and finish up in Andersonstown. It was the average out on the booze on a Friday night after work session and we got progressively more intoxicated as we made our way along. The intelligent thing to do if there can be anything intelligent about a pub crawl is to have a list of Pubs in your head and when you decide your too drunk to continue go to the last pub on your list and finish there so as any stragglers will know where to go if they get separated.

In our case it was the Ex-Servicemen's club past Casement Park and just before the Busy bee Shops. We all ended up there at about 10.00 pm and as we crushed into the last of the free seats the group gave out a stirring rendition of The Boys of the Old Brigade. In the middle of all the commotion I looked up and there was a middle-aged woman standing beside the table next to me and she looked absolutely fed up and bored. I don't know what came over me I mouthed the words do you want to get out of here and she signed back yes. I made my way out and she was waiting at the door, she looked about mid-forties and was small with a nice figure and she was dressed like Suzi Quattro unfortunately that's where the resemblance ended she had a face only a mother could love and showed a broad Belfast inner city accent when she said " What do ya wana do" and with the drink filling me full of Dutch courage I said "well a blow job would do for a start" all right she said as chirpy as a chicken" Mon well head to the Off-licence and you can get us a Big Fuck off carryout". Fast forward Off-licence , Taxi and her house glasses full of Vodka and coke, bra knickers and jocks flung onto the floor and then I looked behind me and there were five or six kids standing there aged from about nine to two just staring at us, "It's all right" says she " they only want to know if you have a car "Jesus Christ with her hand squeezing my cock the way she was I would have told them I had a space ship, they all started talking at once and then yer woman says will you take us all to the seaside in the morning ,Of course I will" I said I'll take you anywhere you want to go now please fuck off. I did everything a man could do in the next hour and by that time I was knackered and had to get a taxi home, I couldn't even put the key in the lock but luckily my Ma heard me and let me in. I woke up in the morning as sick as a dog and with a head like a ruptured melon and the only thing keeping me alive was the power of Paracodol. I lay there with my mouth like the inside of an Arabs sandal and couldn't get back to sleep I had a dredd that something was coming for me but I tried to put the feeling aside and get back to sleep. Then the Dredd came and it was my mother hammering on my bedroom door shouting for me to get up that there was a woman at the door for me. I called my ma up and said in my most pleading voice Please mum tell her I'm sick or not here or something, tell her anything but get rid of her please .My mother looked straight at me and said I'm sure that woman has paid for whatever she wants of you today big time, so I suggest you get up like a big boy and go sort out your own mess. Some of the kids were running around the front garden and some of the others had gone into the house and my Ma was feeding them milk and cookies and yer woman says to me" I thought I come round to your house just in case you forgot the kids are really looking forward to the seaside all the younger have never been Its really awful good of you, you know. By the time I got myself ready the kids were already calling my Ma Granny and she was telling them how cute they were and my Da was sniggering away behind his newspaper. It was a typical Northern Ireland summers day and unfortunately for me it was just good enough to go to the beach. I went out and got in the car and Brenda followed me with her brood who piled cheerfully 5 deep into the back seat of my VW Beetle while she climbed into the front passenger seat with the youngest a 2 year old who constantly cried and blew snotty bubbles all over here baby bottle which she then proceeded to suck with gusto snots and all. I decided to go to Newcastle as I had been there on holiday lots of times and knew my way and I reckoned that I could dump the whole brood in the amusements or on the beach and I could then slope off to some nice little Café were I could spend an hour and get some breakfast, I began to cheer up a bit and I could also get to a pub and have a pint or two and watch the footy on the TV. When we got there I managed to get a nice parking spot on the front of the main street right alongside the Beach. Of course there was a little Sweet and Toy shop not 20 feet from us and the kids jumped out of the car and straight into the shop were they loaded up with Buckets and Spades and Rubber rings while Brenda got sweets and biscuits and juice and walked out leaving me to pay for all of it, then said cheerfully this is great this will do until lunch time and then you can get us all fish and chips. She was serious and I thought she reckoned her ass was made of gold to warrant all this carry on. The kids turned out to be the forty thieves as they stole as much as I was buying and at one stage two of then ran past me being pursued by what I assumed to be an a very irritated shop keeper. The kids and Brenda stuck to me like glue making sure I didn't get anywhere without them and they made certain that I didn't get to spend any money, certainly any money that they didn't get their share of and they were well trained and missed nothing . They genuinely enjoyed the beach and I was nearly sorry to see them go home I said nearly sorry. They were gas little punters and I felt genuinely sorry for them, they thought they were cute and devious but they were as transparent as glass they even had the youngest snotty little one calling me Daddy. If Brenda had'nt been so needy and desperate I might have went out with them again as when I thought about it they were full of life and smiles and their little lives were a million miles from the struggle that was my existence.

I never saw them again and never wanted to but now and again I see their little faces in some nightmare or other I'm having and thank God for my narrow escape. Sometime later friends of mine told me that there was a peculiar aroma wafting around my car although I personally couldn't smell anything but after enough people had told me the same story I gave the car a good search and found a car blanket tied up in a big knot and full of dried shite that my wee beach buddies had left me as a thank you for all my effort on their behalf for our Grand day at the beach. Now and again I hear myself humming "oh hadn't we a jolly good time the day we went to Bangor", and I get a cold shiver as though tiny hands are rummaging through my pockets and the Artfull Dodger and his wee mates have got me cornered and are emptying my pockets while I'm carrying Tiny Tim on my back and look like Bob Crotchet.

The following week was relatively uneventful, we only had one job on and it was pretty straightforward a girl who was in the Cumann Na mBan and worked in a factory down town had accidentally discovered that one of the managers who worked there was an Officer in the UDR and had passed the information on to the local ASU. They checked it out and decided that the information was sound, their only difficulty was that he could only be stiffed in the carpark and because off where he parked his car the shooter would have to walk to him from the getaway car a distance of about 30 yards so obviously he couldn't wear a mask or Balaclava and the target was certain to be armed with his service pistol which he carried all the time. Also as the work force was mixed catholic and protestant any one of the local ASU was certain to be recognised so that meant bringing in an outside shooter which was me. I had a couple of firearms that I liked to keep for just this eventuality ,one was a Colt .45 Auto for its rate of fire and its stopping power and the other an S & W .38 snub nose for back up. As I said before at least I think I said before I liked to use an automatic pistol for close in work but the IRA isn't a conventional army and even if you look after your Fire arm who's to say what Gobshite has used it after you and how old or how badly stored the Ammunition was, I'd already had 3 misfires in CQB and you definitely need back up and what better than a .38 special. I might seem a little blasé about killing another person but the fact is I couldn't give a rats ass about it my main concern is with my safety and freedom that's why the two guns and a driver who was also armed and experienced.

CHAPTER 9:

For all I knew the car park could have been brimming with off duty UDR men, better to be safe than sorry, my Ma didn't raise no fools. The job went off like clockwork we drove in 5 minutes before he was due to leave work and go to his car and when I saw him coming out the doors he was walking by himself. I set off after him and closed the distance to about 20 feet close but not too close as to make the hair on the back of his neck stand up by invading his personal space as well as that we had parked just off to his left which meant that I was coming at him obliquely and wasn't directly behind him. I have learned the lesson of humans and their sixth sense, some people in shootings die oblivious to the danger and yet others seem to realise the imminent danger and you can see their shoulders haunch up and they duck and swivel usually to no avail but sometimes it saves their lives. He didn't realise fuck all and fell with 2 bullets in the back and 1 in the back of his head I was back to the car in a few seconds and we sailed out of the car park and into the city centre and then quickly into safety in the Divis Flats. After dumping the guns and car I jumped a Black Taxi heading up the Falls and when I realised I was well clear I began to wonder what my Ma was making for the dinner I hoped it was stew one of my favourites. I got out near home and was dandering along with my head down when I walked straight into the clutches of a BA foot patrol,well fuck and double fuck They asked me the usual where I was going and I pointed to the house I was only 3 doors away where I was coming from, I said work and gave them my DOB and my ID then they radioed it into base. The sweat was running down my collar and I tried to be as casual as possible I mouthed a silent prayer that the return reply would not be Fresh Meat which would mean a trip to Fort Monagh but thankfully it came back all clear and I was free to go. A few days later I was contacted by 1 st Batt Staff and told to go to what used to be the old A Company area and revitalise it, as all of the volunteers that had previously staffed this Company were either dead or imprisoned, the majority of them were up in Long Kesh. I never knew it was this bad that there wasn't a single member of A Company left in actual fact there were only a handful of girls left in the whole area and there was no resistance left. I was to contact 2 of the girls who were in the Army and apparently there were a number of other girls who were in The Cumann na mBan I had better get this right or even today the same girls would have no problem in stringing you up The Cumann na mBan were the female equivalent of the IRA. The other difference was that some girls were in the Army and they technically out ranked all of the other girls, women for fuck sake they have to complicate everything. Anyway I met the 2 army girls in a safe house in Tullymore Gardens and arranged to get the ball rolling with 4 or 5 quick snipes that could be done with just a couple of people to say to the Japs "well hello boys wear back". The first order of business was to re-arm the Company and get in a small selection of rifles and pistols and some Nail Bombs. Also I found to my horror that I was the only driver in the Company so for some jobs I would have to use a couple of friends of mine from B Company when I needed someone. I started off easy and slow with a snipe down Ramoan Gardens with an Aramlite and one girl to back me up and to take the rifle away to a safe dump after the shot had been fired. I was in a nearby house with the rifle when a Jap foot patrol came out of Gartree place and turned up Ramoan I went out the back door and up to the side of the flats and took one shot down the hill at the Japs .As it turned out I missed but the Japs nearly shit themselves as they weren't used to making contact in the A Company area they had considered pacified. I might have missed but the girls were over the moon mainly because it let the people know that we hadn't been defeated in the A Company area. We followed this up almost immediately with another snipe in Rosnareen Avenue almost a carbon copy of the first one except for the fact that I hit the Jap right in the centre of his chest unfortunately he was carrying his rifle at port arms and the Armalite round went through the back of his hand and lodged in the Butt of his rifle, oh well you win some you lose some but the main thing is to keep punching. Only two days later we set up another snipe from the top of Clonelly Ave at a road block on the Glen Road just at the gates of St Marys School this time there was no miss or bad luck I was using an old friend the .303 Lee Enfield and I shot a soldier who was standing leaning against the wall and blew a hole right through him and knocked a lump out of the wall behind him the size of your fist. It made no difference whether or not he died on the road or died later in hospital or survived, the fact is that he was out of the war for good is enough and in my humble opinion is a job well done. It was all about time , how much of it you had left you never knew and it was soul destroying seeing your mates disappear into Long Kesh as far as you knew for ever or for years you just had to accept that it would happen and do all the damage you could before that day came.

The girls had plenty of experience from before I got there and picked up our Modus Operandi very quickly. I realised that I could use this working between the two Company areas to my advantage as the Brits would find it difficult to understand what had changed and the information they would be getting from the street would be all arseways. The Brits had a very straightforward system which was based to a large degree on informers and what this changing between company's would do was cause their informants to be contradicting themselves by giving the same names doing the same jobs in different areas sometimes on the same day and certainly in the same week. This information would contradict the information they were getting from other sources and they started to disbelieve their informants who started getting nervous and jumpy and the informants began to think that they would get ratted out to the IRA as it so happened two of them handed themselves into the IRA and came clean about what they had been forced to do and the IRA used some of this for publicity purposes and put the informers out of the country for life one got caught because4 he asked too many questions about stuff that did'nt concern him and one of them got caught because he asked too many questions about areas he should have had no interest in or contact with.

In the meantime a potential job came up that we couldn't afford to miss. One of our Fianna volunteers had discovered a path across the roof of De La Salle school apparently they were up on the roof at night spying on the ladies keep fit classes who used the gym and the showers to of course, dirty little feckers . They discovered that you could get from the front of the school to the back by using a little pathway that ran between the buildings and the front of the school and over looked the back gate of Silver City one of the Brit forts in Andytown and the path brought you back to Knockdhu Park a street which ran along the rear of the school. The Brits when starting their daily patrols almost always sent their first patrol out the back gate and onto Edenmore Drive which brought them into our field of fire from the school roof. It was necessary to do the job on a Saturday or preferably a Sunday when the school would be empty and the whole area would be locked up. So on a Thursday night three of us went to the back gates of the school and using the Hydraulic Jack from the boot of my car, spread the railings beside the gate so as we could squeeze through one at a time. The next step was to check the path across the roof and find out how difficult it was and were abouts it brought us at the front of the school. We came across a couple of problems one it was a fucking long long way from front to back, well over 200 yds secondly the roof heights were un even and this meant climbing up and down 3 to 4 sections of wall however the canter of the roof ran down slope from front to back which made it easier for us to runback after the shooting also we could take our time getting to the firing position as the

Brits couldn't see us and the front edge of the roof was a four foot wall. Two other difficulty's presented themselves one was there was a six foot gap between two sections of the school and the drop was about 20ft so we had to be careful with our long jump there if you fell down there you were   fucked and even if you hadn't broken anything there was no way out.

So our runback consisted of a 200 yrd dash back across the roof of the school with a single story long jump over the gap and then a single story jump off the roof to land on the grassy bank beside the school. Then we had an 100 yrd run across the back yard and squeeze through the spreaded bar beside the gate and then another 100 yard dash up the little lane that ran up the side of Knockdhu Park and into a broad parking area that lay at the back of Gartree Place in which we would leave our getaway car. I was going to drive the getaway car myself which would save on manpower and do the Shooting with the other volunteer who would work with me on the job. I picked the two weapons for the shooting an SLR for me and an AR 180 for my comrade, the SLR was captured when a Brit sped off in an open jeep and dropped his rifle after he had taken a bullet in a fire fight a few months earlier.

CHAPTER 10:

On Sunday Morning when the rest of Ireland was at Mass we were taking possession of an old but reliable Austin Cambridge for our getaway and after checking there were no Helicopters around I parked it in the getaway position. Again there were no choppers up or at least visible so my buddy and I decided we would'nt need masks as with any luck the only Brits we would see would be down the barrels of our guns. We both wore Parkas and as it was fairly mild outside we were both sweating heavily as we jogged down the passage way squeezed through the railing climbed up a drainpipe onto the roof and made our way over the roof to our firing position. I'd say that we were only waiting about half an hour when I saw movement at the back gates and a small figure sprinted out the gates to the side wall of the end house in Edenmore drive we waited until three or four of them had moved from cover to cover along the street and then I said to my Buddy ,Right I'll fire first and then you pick a target and put as many rounds into him as you can and remember you have 20 rounds there keep five for the runback in case anything goes wrong. As it turned out it was a prophetic statement on my part as I was about to find out. I took aim on a Brit silhouetted in an entry doorway and squeezed the trigger. There was a bang followed by long burst of fire as my buddy let off his whole magazine in one continuous rip he had no fully auto on his AR180 but he managed to kill a number of slates on the rooves opposite. I continued on firing counting off the rounds in my head the Brit in the alleyway door had disappeared and I re sighted after each shot and fired at a number of targets until I had reached 14 rounds and much as I was tempted in the face of such a target rich environment I stopped and took off back on our runback over the school roof I could hear the Brits returning fire and as no bullets could come our way because of the angle of the building I could only imagine the number of windows getting murdered in the front of the school it must have been carnage on a shattering level. I caught up on my buddy as he had slowed down as he approached the long jump across the passage way and as I ran past him I shouted jump or die and he took the leap just after me and just teetering on the edge of the drop managed to gain his balance and pull himself together and continue running. I silently prayed to God that we had stiffed a few of the bad guys and that this had not been a waste of time. I knew that at more than 200 yds your foresight obscures your target who is taking cover and giving you not a lot to aim at and that counting your chickens was a waste of time. The pair of us dashed across the schools roof without looking back and I again outpaced him and when I got to the edge of the building I threw myself headlong of the roof and holding my gun out in front of me landed with a thud on the grass bank I was on my feet in an instant and heading for the spread railing it wasn't a pretty jump I never claimed to land like a paratrooper I landed more like a sack of spuds. I took a look for my pal who should have been right behind me but instead he was hanging off the edge of the building by the lanyard of his rifle which was caught on the down pipe on the wall , he obviously didn't jump but had slung the rifle across his back and tried to climb down but had gotten stuck on the edge of the roof unable as the little rhyme says and when he was up he was up but as the Grand Old Duke of York says he was neither up nor down. I felt like leaving him and for a second I nearly did but instead I ran back to him and got below his feet and after a minute or two managed to get him down. I was fucking fuming because I knew we were bolloxed, I told him to run for it as I could hear a chopper coming and I knew it would be over us in a couple of seconds I knew it was too late as we ran up the little lane at the side of the street and then I felt the downdraft on the back of my neck and I spun around and saw a what we called a Bubbly Copter the one with the little clear plastic cockpit. It was only about 30 feet above us and this bollox was hanging out of the side door with a Sterling Sub Machine gun pointed directly at me I fired first and because of the angle he was at I gave him two rounds up the Khyber Pass for his cheek and followed up with two more rounds into the cockpit in general to make sure he fucked off which he did but I heard a grinding crash somewhere behind me and I realised he must have come down. I tore out of the lane and saw my buddy in the car getting it started I pulled him out by the collar and shouted out to him It's too late for that get into somebody's house quick, your own your own now good luck and as I said that a Saracen armoured car came around the corner at the top of the hill and opened fire on us. There were thuds and thuds and thuds holes appeared all over our getaway car which with lumps of metal flying of it had got its last getaway. The last I saw of our gallant car it was down on its axles and looked totally poleaxed. I ran into the maze of back gardens in Gartree Place and quickly checked each back door as I ran along the row of houses. I found one and went in and quietly locked the door behind me there was a whole large family in the house all boys I could tell this as they were all kneeling along the settee which was in front of the living room window and the lot of them were lined along the length of it looking at the hell breaking loose out on the street, I coughed loudly from behind them and they turned around to find themselves looking at a fine figure of a man, me I mean with a rifle across my chest. The wee ones cheered and I told them to get back from the window and be quiet because the Brits were coming and we didn't want to draw attention to the house. The older ones copped on and in double quick time everybody was either watching TV or reading comics

I explained to the woman of the house that I was in a desperate situation and I had no choice but than to use her house for cover I promised her that if the Brits came that I wouldn't turn her house into a shooting gallery but that I would surrender and explain that I had forced them to take me in and hide the gun and I assured her I would take responsibility for the lot. My next order of business was to hide the gun so with the two older lads following me I went upstairs and looked for one of the boys bedrooms that had Bunk Beds and then broke down the SLR into two sections the forearm stock with the barrel and the Butt with the mouse I then lifted up the mattress on one of the top bunks and threw a sheet of the bed over the bed boards and covered it with the mattress, it was the best I could come up with at that moment in time. I went back down stairs took off my parka jacket and told the Ma to calm down if we got raided I would pretend to be her eldest son and if they found me out then I would surrender. I didn't want anybody to look out the window or peek out of the curtains in case it attracted unwelcome attention to the house. The Brits were having a field day outside and there were sporadic bursts of gunfire echoing up and down the street. I got the impression that the Brits at either end of the street were shooting at each other a sort of double friendly fire I wondered who would win. After a little while the shooting stopped and we heard the shouting and cursing of Brit voices outside on the street and very close to the door. The TV was playing loudly and when I turned it down so as I could hear what was going on outside the younger kids complained and created a fuss and I had to turn the volume up again. I told the two older boys to make tea for their Ma and me because her face was very pale and I was afraid of her passing out or having a fit or something worse. Worse it was she was pacing up and down the living room muttering to herself O Jesus ,O Jesus O Jesus and wringing her hands and I thought if a Brit looks in the window and sees this carry on I'm fucked. Then she started having a seizure and I looked for somewhere to put her but all three rooms downstairs had big windows so there was nowhere to put her that the Brits couldn't see her I looked over at the kids and the littler ones were just about ready to roar and bawl so I gave up and decided to try and move to another house, easier said than done. As soon as I voiced my intention to leave the Ma was all too eager to help she told me to go upstairs and get the gun and that she would go out to the front door and check if it was all clear. When I was stuffing the two halves of the gun under the armpits of my parka one of the older lads told me he was sorry and was ashamed at his Ma's carry on .I went down and stood at the front door and told her to check the front door once more and see what the story was she did this and told me to go now, I stepped outside and she closed the door behind me. I stood with my back to the door and felt the pit of my stomach sink through to my Anus.There were Brits everywhere there were 2 on my right hand side and 1 on my left and 2 standing at the bottom of the garden path how apt I thought I had been lead up the garden path and I was now up shite creek without a paddle as far as I'm concerned I think there's no better time for a cliché than when you are Royally screwed.

I walked down the path and I was sure they were going to stop me and they did, they then started to ask me the usual questions and finished up asking me to produce my identity it went through my head to say (surely officer, and would you kindly hold this rifle for me while I get it for you). I just stood there looking at them not knowing what to do and unable to do anything. Then a big burly man appeared in our midst and pushing the Brits aside he punched one in the face and he began to boot the head off the other one. Brits came running from everywhere and I slipped away walking quickly up the street past Brits who seemed to be in every second garden. About another 20 to 30 houses later I was stopped by one of our Fianna Boys who lived in that street and he mouthed to me to follow him into the house. I did and when I got in the young Fianna Boy took the rifle and said I' I'll get rid of this'. So I took my coat off rolled up my shirt sleeves and started to think about what I was going to do to get out of this. The mother said that they would hide the gun in the kitchen and fit it down the back of a built in table and they took the bulb out of one of the kitchen lights The woman told me to wait until the Brits came to search the house and when I asked why she was so certain the house would get raided she stated simply that it always did. About half an later they came thundering up the path and burst into the house, I waited about two minutes and then stood up and set my cup of tea down on the arm of the chair and said listen Ma I'm nipping over to Johns house I want to borrow some of his after shave and stuff for going out tonight I'll see you in about five minutes. OK sunshine she said I'll see you in a minute. This was a watershed moment there were 3 brits standing in the living room and I had to walk past them to get out the door I didn't say anything to them to encourage eye contact but just sauntered past them and straight into the house facing them on the other side of the road The householder was waiting at the door for me he had watched the whole show from his bedroom window and was ready in case he could help. His daughter put her coat on and together we walked down to the end of the back garden and I said thanks I can take it from here, no way she was letting me go on my own so we climbed over the back hedge and into a different garden and house in a different street we had ended up in Knockdhu Park the street where the whole shooting match had begun. She walked with me until we were well clear of the Brits and I thanked her and went on my way. I made my way back to our safe house and they were astonished to see me they thought I was dead and then not 20 minutes later in walked my partner in crime. I sent the girls for a carry out and then we all sat down to relax my own story was wild enough but his had got to be better when he started of his story with the words , 'I was sitting on the bog having a shite when this Brit burst in' there were howls of laughter as he told his tale though he didn't mention what had gotten us into the terrible situation in the first place and I let it go as we had need of something to lighten the evening which turned into a holey and I woke up the next morning with a splitting head and a naked girl in my bed and I couldn't remember anything so instead of having an awkward conversation I got dressed and took myself off .

I went down town to the Markets area of Belfast to stay with my Granny for a couple of weeks as I was beginning to feel under pressure in Andytown and anyway I have always liked the Markets there was always plenty to do and lots of watering holes between there and The Short Strand. I met up with a couple of my old buddies and we went out on the tare in the city centre although we were careful about the pubs and clubs we frequented but it made a big change in my lifestyle and I was able

to relax. The Markets and the Strand were in the 3rd Battalion area of the Belfast Brigade and they had seen their fair share of fighting but as in any small area the Brits get to know the operators and you run into the problem that when you do a job locally you know the Brits will be coming for you and you have to arrange an alibi as well as do the job this makes life twice as difficult and takes all the fun out of the game. So here was I a relative stranger and ideally placed to pull off a job and all the locals had to do was make sure that they all had good alibis. They hadn't been able to pull off a successful job in about four months and they were worried that they were letting the pressure on the Brits slip. Although ambushes were not really their forte what they were best at was defending their area against attack by the thousands of Orangemen that lived in the surrounding streets. From my standpoint I was happy to oblige the lads by doing the shooting for them and I only had to worry about the actual job itself and I didn't have to worry about being connected with the ambush as nobody knew me. They didn't waste any time and had a car stolen and an old terrace house which backed onto Cromac Sq set up and ready and an AK 47and Baretta Sub Machine gun a model 38 a world war two relic which I was assured was in perfect working order. I had never seen one and the two triggers for fully auto and single shot put me off however I didn't have to use it that was the backup shooters job mine was to hit up an RUC jeep and pour 7.62 rounds in through the open back doors and hit as many Peelers as possible. I was never any great expert on motorcars and although I drove one I just expected it to go and stop and not break down, I only ever put petrol in it and I can't honestly recall If I ever put oil in it at all somebody told me that VW Beetles ran forever and I took that literally anyway this was a blue Cortina which meant absolutely nothing to me other than it was blue. The old terrace house on the other hand was truly a piece of Markets nostalgia, it was a one up and one down with brick shit house in the back yard that was full of broken gutters and weeds. It was decorated in the late religious style with pictures of the Pope, JFKennedy and The Sacred Heart with wee electric bulbs on them you know the type that never burn out at that time it was the Irish Holy Trinity. The whole place was mouse infested and semi derelict and just for good measure had a gaping hole in the roof were a half dozen of the slates had slipped off and landed in the yard. I recall the name for them was Bangor Blues I knew this because an old Aunt of mine had lost a couple of slates of her roof in more ways than one and my Ma had volunteered me to fix it and I had major problems in getting replacements until in the end I borrowed them off another house when the occupants were on holiday.

By about 2.00pm we were just finishing checking over the weapons over when something that had been bugging me just suddenly formed in my head the lights on the Sacred Heart Pictures were on that meant there was electricity and we had been told that the house was abandoned and derelict then I heard footsteps on the stairs and in an instant I had pivoted around and dropped to one knee with my rifle pointing at the door. The footsteps got closer and I took first pressure on the trigger and then to my amazement and relief some doddery oul fella came into the bedroom with an arm load of Holy Pictures clutched to his chest, muttering to himself something Holy Jesus as he took a picture of the Pope down from above the bed, looked sideways at us and said yous are a pack of Heathens this was holy Gods House ,good luck and god bye as he made his way back down stairs and out the door. My buddy looked at me and said, Surreal by fuck and turned to the window without another word. The two of us were there nearly an hour when something even more surreal than the previous surreal took place I was aiming out the window and idly placing the foresight of my rifle on pedestrians ,as you do when you're bored when I realised that I was aiming at the back of my Granny's head I was shocked to see my old Aunt and her Handicapped Nephew making their way across Cromac Sq on their way to daily mass in St Malachys Chapel, how many people have pointed a gun at their Granny's head for any reason Fucking Surreal. Back to business and 10mins later the promised RUC Jeep sailed sedately into Cromac Sq with the back doors wide open and Peelers nearly hanging out the back of it I shouted fire and we fired together me on the AK slowly and steadily placing every round into the heaving mass of black clothed bodies and my buddy firing steady 3 to 4 round bursts into the carnage. The sound inside the bedroom was deafening and as we ran down the stairs I pulled a cigarette butt out of each ear that's a great idea he roared into my face as he couldn't hear anything. The car, the Blue car, was there waiting on us and the driver drove us slowly and carefully out of the Markets and into the Strand and safety.

No harm to most of my Comrades in A'Town but it was nice to work with professionals for a change it gives you more confidence and helped ensure that the little errors in judgement didn't happen as often. I spent the rest of my little holiday in the Pubs and clubs getting drink sent over from people I didn't know ,one of whom was Silver Mc Kee a great oul Markets character and a gentleman depending on who you talk to . He was a great street fighter in his day and beat the shit out of Peelers, Orangemen and assorted dirty bums that crossed his path, I won't go into Silvers exploits as I could end up with too much to deal with at any one time. Anyway if you spend too long in an area as small as the Markets, people start to ask too many questions about who you are where you come from and what you're doing there. So it was slan to my wee mid- summer break and back to business.

Just coincidentally it was my small sojourn in the Markets that led to my involvement in one of the biggest bomb attacks that Belfast had ever experienced up to that time. As the job in the Markets had gone so well the Brigade Staff seconded me to the local Markets ASU again to take part in what was to take place the following week. I don't remember being consulted on the matter, just told to report in ASAP. I wasn't very keen on this turn of events it was one thing to volunteer for an operation and quite another to be volunteered. Anyway there was sod all else for us to do at that particular time as the IRA had called a Ceasefire and we were all stood down temporarily until whatever was happening had happened. Funny enough the MRF choose this day to raise their ugly heads when they shot 4 men at a Bus Stop on the Glen Road claiming that they had been fired upon and had lawfully returned fire. It was a carbon copy of our shoot and scoot the only difference being that if these Boyo's had been caught they would have been given a medal and not twenty years in the Maze. The ceasefire only lasted about a month and culminated in the Lenadoon Gun battle which put us all back in business again. Later I found that the bombing for which I had been selected was definitely on the cards and I was told to drop everything else get my arse down to the Markets were I would be briefed. I did try and explain that I knew sweet FA about bombs but I was told that I would only be the Driver and there would be somebody from the Bomb squad with me who knew the score. I had already planted a couple of bombs and I didn't like it one of the bombs blew up a small car rental firm but the other one was a total fuck up, one of the girls and myself took a 25lb satchel bag into the city centre and were told to plant the bomb as near to any BA personnel or Police as we could. The bomb was already primed and on its 2 hr countdown. Two hours should have been enough time to plant the thing bomb but we kept getting moved on by the cops and couldn't get a clear spot to dump it. At this moment time was off the essence we looked around desperately and spotted the only place available ,it was a trendy little restaurant and the Cops were nowhere near it at that point in time, we went upstairs and I asked the girl with me if she wanted a drink or something but she whispered to me ' we 've got to get the fuck out of here before it's too late' there was no way I was arguing it was her call as she was on the bomb squad and technically outranked me on a job like this. Needless to say we walked out into that grey overcast sky and kept going until we got up to Royal Ave when we heard the thud of the explosion it wasn't particularly loud as exploisons go but we had an idea that the 2 of us were going to get the rounds of the kitchen when we eventually got back to Battalion staff to report in. So myself and herself caught a pre-arranged lift and went back to an empty call house in A 'Town and went to bed. I slept for nearly two hours solid and then went to sleep and I dreamed of a little Cumman na mBan girl and the things I would do to her the next chance I got. That night we heard it on the 6,00 pm news and to be honest with you it was'nt as bad as I thought there were only a couple of people killed and a lot injured so I gave my conscience a rest and decided given the circumstances it was a better outcome than we could have hoped for.

Ever since the escapade with the bombing of the restraunt I had managed to stay clear of the bomb squad and their cunning plans and managed to stick with what I knew best any way I got no satisfaction out of blowing places up operations like that didn't get the adrenaline flowing. However refusing to turn up for an operation that you had been ordered to attend wasn't an option either. So I toddled off down the Markets to find out what my part was in the upcoming events. It's hard to rationalise your feelings when an operation of this size is outlined for you and it's especially difficult when you are experienced enough to know that in a job of this size and complexity that something is always bound to go wrong. My task was to drive one of the bomb cars from the Markets to the intended target which was less than 500 yards away and park it there after immobilising the engine and taking the car key. The bomb was already primed and set to explode 2 hours later my partner and I planted our bomb as quickly as we could then walked back to the Markets and told the Operation co-ordinator where exactly the car had been parked and everything was set. With my part finished I walked out of the Markets up to Castle St and caught a bus home. I was back in Andytown before the first Bomb had gone off and as the news came trickling in of the amount of death and destruction that had resulted I decided to stay in that Friday night and not go out with the lads as usual as the only topic of conversation would be about the bombings and I was in no mood to discuss it.

The phone rang constantly however with my mates calling and telling me to get off my arse and come out for the night and in the end I gave up got myself ready and headed out. I enjoyed drinking in Broadway and the Beehive in particular was one of my favourite pubs. The common story was that you were searched for knives on the way in and if you hadn't got one they gave you one but we knew this wasn't true as the Bouncers in the Beehive knew better than to attempt to search the type of clientele that frequented the place. The Beehive was always the last pub we hit at the end of the night as they sold Carry outs for when you just had to have that very last Gargle that turned your legs to rubber. It was no coincidence we finished up in Beechmount as one of the lads lived there with his Ma and Da and a space on the rug in front of the fire was always available. One night we were really pissed and fell asleep in front of the fire as usual there were 4 of us and when we awoke the next morning our shoes were missing. I went into the kitchen following the aroma of frying bacon and found the Oul Fella cooking breakfast good man I said I'm starving by the way did you happen to see our shoes, ' O yea he says I burned them' . I was absolutely Gobsmacked who in the name of fuck would even think of that ,what sort of an arsehole would burn your shoes , Oh its getting cold in here lets be having your shoes boys, if he'd said he was frying up the family dog I'd have believed him.

I was getting used on too many jobs and I had a feeling in my water that unless I slowed down a bit I was going to get croaked or locked up in Long Kesh. It's a sobering thought to realise that your time is running out so I decided to back off the operations for a month or two even the 2 weeks I had spent in the Markets I had to trade in for killings. So I said nothing and just slowed down I put my time into training the girls and in all honestly they picked it up very quickly of course they had been supporting IRA operations for a long time . The Brits either didn't know them or didn't rate them because they very seldom arrested them or seemed to think that without a man around they couldn't cause much bother how wrong they were. The first order of business was to set up a list of operations that we could work through instead of taking jobs ad hoc. This would enable us to plan in advance and have the right weapons and personnel available for specific operations. Also the girls had a limited range of tasks they could perform but the big limiting factor they all had was that they couldn't shoot for shit; whilst they had all the courage in the world they had no real proficiency with firearms. They had invaluable resources they had safe houses, call houses, arms dumps and access to a whole cadre of well-trained scouts. I set up a rota for irregular meetings were we could receive and pass on intelligence on the identity of security force personnel and movements of British army units. The kids on the streets saw everything and missed nothing a good example of the success of this strategy was the taking down of an MRF/SAS undercover operation called The Four Square Laundry, which ran a Laundry delivery and collection service in the Twinbrook Area of West Belfast. Over a period of months the girls had discovered that the Service was in fact an MRF/SAS sting and they were actually collecting information on the IRA in the local area, they also discovered that the MRF/SAS had another business on the Antrim Road in Belfast called Gemini Health Studio which was ostensibly a massage parlour. The cheek of the bastards was unbelievable and we took it out a couple of months later. An ASU from Lenadoon and Twinbrook took out the van killing 3 SAS operatives and narrowly missing a female undercover operative who was away from the van at the time picking up laundry heard the shooting and legged it to safety into a local house where she spun the occupant a cock and bull story and they believing her put her in contact with the security forces. The Gemini Health Studio we took out ourselves killing the 2 SAS operatives on duty at the time. Although we claimed the operation and the 5 dead SAS operatives the Brits never admitted this serious loss of intelligence personnel until many years later when the ITV or the BBC ran a documentary on the whole show and even then the Brits tried to keep the truth of their losses to a minimum. It was the biggest loss of life the SAS had suffered since WW2. Needless to say they weren't happy chappies in Hereford or traipsing the mountains with a 90lb Bergen on your back felt pretty useless with the knowledge that a few ill trained Mickey Mousers from Belfast could take them out so easily.

It's hard to describe our lifestyle in those days to most people, it was like it was like operating and living behind enemy lines we were constantly stopped and P Checked, searched, insulted and getting physically abused. Not to mention constant arrest and interrogation by the Brits and the RUC. I noticed that the Brits and the RUC didn't willingly pass on on information to each other but always seemed to be at loggerheads. Also they raided our house on a regular basis about once or twice a month, it got to the stage that my mother didn't bother tacking the carpets as they were lifted so often there was no point. The number of close calls we had was unbelievable; on one occasion we called at one of the girls houses to collect her for a night out, my friend and his girlfriend and myself. We were only in the house for a minute when it was raided by the Brits who held us at gunpoint while they P Checked us and searched the house. A young soldier was left to cover us and the woman of the house offered us all tea including the Brit alarm bells rang with me immediately as we were barely civil with the Brits never mind giving them tea, what the fuck was she playing at . She went around telling everybody to sit down and relax and when she got close to me she mouthed the word' Look' and I followed her gaze to a man's suit that was hanging up on the pelmet rail on the living room wall. The Brit was too fucking sharp and as he caught her look he strode across the room in an instant and pulled the jacket open revealing an AR180 hanging underneath it, I had a split second chance to go for him and grab the gun but I hesitated and he brought the rifle to his shoulder and pointed it directly at my chest I thought it was all over when to my utter amazement he brought his finger to his lips in a shush motion and stepped back to his place by the door. I wondered what the hell he was up to then he gave me a conspiratorial smile and said nothing to his comrades so they never found the weapon sometimes the oddest of things can happen and there never seems to be any rhyme or reason to them I still wonder today what possessed that soldier to act the way he did don't get me wrong I was extremely grateful that he did only for him my budding terrorist career would have come to an abrupt end. It was on occasions like this that I would have preferred to have fought along the border at least there when you weren't operational you could relax on the

Free State sider. It was for this reason that we went down south any weekend we could manage were we could drink and howl and chase women to our hearts content. My favourite place for R&R was Cork City and County basically as far from the Border and the Brits as it was possible to get in Ireland. They called it the rebel county and the pubs were alive every night with the craic and Diddly Dee music and all the people were friendly and Republican. It was also helpful that I had a cousin who lived in a small village in West Cork called Ballincollig and she put us up with no hesitation or questions asked and we kept everyone in the house supplied with copious amounts of alcohol. It was there on a night out I was introducedto an elderly man sitting alone in the pub and just drinking tea, she asked me if I recognised him and I did and she introduced us to him , it was Tom Barry the commander of the West Cork Flying Colum during the war of Independence. We offered him a drink but he declined as he was a Pioneer and hadn't taken a drink of alcohol in years. He was avid for first hand news of the war in the North and questioned us with a shrewd intellect on everything we could tell him.

CHAPTER 11:

He was ruthless in his day and encouraged us to do the same he told us first-hand about the Kilmichael ambush in the 1920's were his Flying Colum ambushed and killed 16 British Soldiers. His attitude was tough and uncompromising and I wouldn't have liked to have fought against him.

In all the talks we had with him he was very candid and open with us the most worrying thing I remember him saying to us was 'I suppose you realise that you are very likely to be killed up there and that you will never win against the British because they have no honour and are dissemblers and liars they will suck the life from you. The best advice I can give to you is Noli Illegitimi Carborundum' (don't let the bastards grind you down) He died in 1980having lived long enough to see his record broken at Narrow Water. On our way home we rang ahead to check how things were and we were told all clear so when we arrived it was straight to bed to sleep of the drink and in my case be fit for work the next morning. I spent the next week in work making up lost time and the evenings working on our weapons cache loading magazines, cleaning guns and making nail bombs and petrol bombs you know all the little mundane tasks that keep the wolf from the door or in our case the Japs.

The following weekend my best friend who had joined the Irish Army some time previous and was now a Caporal came up from Dundalk Army Barracks where he was stationed to see me visit his mother who lived across the road from me and to get a weekend out in Belfast. He called to my house and my mother told him that I was out but she gave him the address of a house that I was using at the time and not knowing any different he made his way up to see me. I was stunned when he appeared at the door and I got him in pronto in case the Brits spotted him. He looked the archetypical picture of a soldier with his tightly cropped hair and little moustache and if the Brits had seen him they most surely would have pulled him in because he looked out of place walking around Andytown. I reassured the rest of the people in the house that he was ok and that I would look after him. I got him a cup of tea it was only then when he went into the kitchen that he saw the weapons sitting around all over the place. He said oh fuck I'm sorry I'll get out of here and see you in your Ma's later, unfortunately it was already too late as one of the girls informed me that there were Brits standing around the house. I could see that he had got very nervous and that he was starting to stress out so I told him not to worry and I gave him a fully loaded FN rifle and told him to stick with me in case of any trouble. Once he was told what to do he settled down I explained to him that this particular house had never been raided and there was no reason for anything bad to happen. So we moved the weapons behind the downs stairs doors were they couldn't be seen from the ground floor windows I winked at him and when he gave me a smile I knew that he would be alright and I knew he was no coward and would fight like hell. I wasn't particularly worried there were 3 volunteers including myself and 2 girls who once they could get out the doors would disappear down into the Estate. It turned out in the end that everything blew over and the Japs moved off and myself and my buddy sauntered off down to my ma's house to get fed and cleaned up. The Club of choice for most of us if you were lucky enough to be out with a woman was the Green Briar just off the Glen Road. It had started life as a Golf Driving range but the owner Noel Boyle added on two function rooms a restaurant and then applied for a Drink and Nightclub licence.

The whole notion of a Golf Driving range in Andytown was a joke there can't have been more than 200 people played golf in the whole of Andytown most of them were Priests, Doctors and a few professional people who lived on the outskirts of the estate. The Briar as we called it was split in two a Large Disco hall and a smaller Ballad Lounge I went to either of the halls depending on whether or not I was looking for a woman or already had one with me. I remember sitting perfectly still as the group played some of our favourite Rebel Songs and sitting there as still as possible to prove how Macho you were, looking back we were such assholes. The girls had arranged to meet us there my usual squeeze and a friend she had brought for my mate, they usually met us outside and we paid them in and and stood the costs for the night never let it be said that a woman had to put her hand in her pocket when I took them out. I was old school in so far as if you took a girl out on a date you paid for everything from taxis and admission to drinks and food. I liked the Briar also because you were relatively safe because there were always a couple of girls with pistols sitting in the audience on protection duty just in case an assassination attempt was made by the Loyalists or undercover brit murder squads. British Army foot patrols usually made an appearance once or twice during the night and came around the tables P Checking some of the patrons. They didn't usually pull people out of the clubs as this often led to hand to hand fighting in the isles and murder on the dance floor. On occasion there were humorous interchanges between the Brits and members off the audience like when there was a black soldier among the BA patrol and when to our delight some wag would shout' hey blackie yer mas in bed with a big nigger' to which the black soldier would shout back in a real Jamaican accent I should hope so Mon that be my Da'. Or the group would sing a really provocative rebel song and then shout remember our name were the – and then they would give the name of a rival Rebel Group. Sometimes a Brit would get up onstage and belt out an Elvis song and take a bow much to the delight of the crowd. About a couple of hours into the night a friend of mine came over to me and told me that some lads at the Bar had discovered that my mate was an Irish Soldier and they were going to shoot him. I went up to see what was going on and it was more serious than I thought, there were 2 assholes one of them armed with a Colt .45 pistol and they were in the process of taking my mate outside to shoot him. I knew one of them they were in the Auxies but they didn't know me which was how it was supposed to be but didn't leave me in a position of authority in a situation like this. I got between them and told them what I was and threatened them with death if they touched him. I stood between them and blocked them from taking a shot. I had no choice then but to jump on one grab the gun and take him down with a fast Uchi Mata and as he hit the ground I twisted the firearm from his grasp when in jumps one of the girls who was carrying a bottle of Jack Daniels we had bought for later and smashed it over the other punters head. The bottle smashed and the drink went everywhere, there was a dead silence among some of the bystanders then somebody said 'fuck me she's after smashing a bottle of whiskey over his head and it was full' ,to which there was an awed silence.

Altough my mate never let on that this incident affected him in any way he went back down to Dundalk the next day and I never saw him again for nearly a year. It was due to this nonsense that I ran into a friend of my mates who had heard about the goings on in the Briar and came to see me to check he had got home all right and while he was talking to me he casually let slip that he might have a place were we could dump guns and while we had a good number of dumps this one was an old Housing Trust Garage in a small row which were vacant and had fallen into disuse. The original idea I think behind building them was to afford private parking for people who were car owners in the sixty's and didn't mind walking to the end of the street to park their car in a locked and secure environment but like all of these fancy ideas they were great on paper and didn't work in reality. They ended up getting vandalised and you may as well have written a note to every hood in Andytown that there was something of value kept here. Twig as his nickname implied was tall and stick thin with a handful of spikey hair sticking out at all angles. His girlfriend was wheelchair bound but they got on like a house on fire and she had a great personality funny enough he met her in the Green Brair one night when he blocked out of his head. She was sitting back against the wall and when he asked her to dance she pointed to the Wheelchair to see if he was taking the piss.Twig however was not to be put off and came back with a quick riposte ' Well can I wheel you home' and they had been going steady ever since. So I made arrangements to meet Twig at the Garage to check it out but it was fit for nothing there were holes in the roof and bricks missing out of the wall and the big swing door didn't swing anymore and there was a couple of big turds in the corner were some Gentleman or Lady had taken a big dump. I told Twig that it was no good and he was visibly disappointed. As we walked away he said' I'm sorry for wasting your time those Garages are only fit for demolishing'. I took a last look at them as we dandered away and the germ of an idea ran through my head maybe there was a use for them and like Baldric I had a cunning plan.

I got a couple of the lads together and we had a good look at the possibility of pulling off the operation I had thought of and the more we looked at it the more feasible it seemed. The garages were right at the junction of two streets forming a tee junction which was overlooked across a small valley called Chalky Field the far side of which was bordered by a row of houses. When we checked them out there were about 4 houses that had a good field of fire across Chalkey and down onto the tee junction a distance of about 150 yards that was far enough for us if anything 150 yards was as far as I could shoot accurately so it was possible to shoot a Brit and use his body as bait to draw the Brits into raiding the garages one of which was going to be booby trapped with

a fifteen or twenty pond bomb. There was one minor difficulty our Battalion EO was too fond of spending his time in the Boozer and was hard to pin down to a time that we could plan for and we had to keep on his back constantly to get and keep him with the programme. He eventually got his act together and got in touch with me to arrange to plant the booby trap bomb, he said that I should come and help him as he needed one other person to complete the installation and as I already knew about the operation there was no need to bring in anyone else. I wasn't a fuckin happy bunny I tell you as I had no faith in this asshole to wire up the garage without killing us both. However I turned up that night and had already set the job up with the rest of the team for the following day. We had a car stolen and the house and family organised to be taken hostage and we had to do it fairly shortly as we would be leaving the Booby trapped garage with no protection in case one of the local kids tried to break in for pure vandalism and blew himself to eternity. Now it was time to plant the bomb and I was already there on watch and armed with a pistol in case the Brits interrupted us and we had to shoot our way out. Then your man arrives with a Donkey jacket on him and carrying a metal pipe the size of a golf bag, I said' what the fuck size of a bomb is that' and he told me not to worry it may look like a 100 lb bomb but the explosive was low grade Nitro Benzene mix and it would only have the power of a 15 lb bomb. 'Trust me' he said but to say I was dubious was an understatement. He then shoved the pipe through the hole in the wall and hauled himself in after it I asked him half-heartedly if he needed my help in there and breathed a sigh of relief when he said no you just keep watch outside and if anything happens don't you dare fuck off and leave me. The next minute he starts sawing, hammering, dragging stuff around dropping stuff cursing and swearing flashing a light on and off and generally acting like a bull I in a china shop. This went on for what seemed hours but was only in reality about fifteen minutes and I was sweating buckets in pure terror that the ejit would blow both of us up. Just then his face appeared at the hole and he stuck his arm out and told me to grab it and help to pull him through I asked him if he still had to do the hole from the outside and he told me not to be silly that the door and the hole were already done. Then he got stuck and I was pulling and he was struggling and I realised that the bomb was live I gave one last heave and he wriggled clear of the hole and I said' thank Jesus", you fat arsehole you could have blown both of us to kingdom come ' and he said 'who are you calling an arsehole' this wasn't Jesus we were calling a fat asshole but the other fat asshole really thought Jesus was a fat asshole oh! Fuck forget about the whole Jesus thing entirely.I stayed off the drink and socialising that night as in fact I did on nearly any night when I had an operation on for the next day. I was always wound up before a job and usually found it hard to sleep, instead I tossed and turned and questioned why I was laying worried sick I questioned why I should be doing this and why not someone else. Finally I came to the conclusion that I was an excitement junkie. Every time I thought that I had all the reasons sussed I would get into the same position again and come up with another set of answers. So the next morning I was up bright and early got a good breakfast into me, you know start the day off right so you can do wrong. Take a long deep breath of the fresh morning air and wrap yourself in your cloak of invincibility. To go and kill or be killed and all this worry and stress was self-inflicted. I couldn't think off one good reason to continue to do this , I didn't hate the Brits much as I tried, I didn't love Ireland as much as I should.I also hated to see the Butchers Apron flying high over my country and the sight of their cheeky uniforms as they marched around .

CHAPTER 12:

I think it was the uniforms. There were only 3 of us on the job, myself and the driver to take the house and hold the family hostage and the third man as a scout from his vantage point at the top of the hill he could see the whole area clearly and he had a whistle which he could blow if he spotted any Jap patrols he looked the part and was wearing a football kit to go with his wee whistle and as it turned out he got stopped after the job and the japs assuming he was a genuine player and the fact that he was wearing a Man Utd rig gave him the look of a normal young lad out for a game of footie on a Saturday morning. Things like this were encouraged they gave you the normalcy factor and the Japs fell for it every time. The amount of times I wore a three piece suit with a pocket watch in the waistcoat waltzed me through many a check point when the Japs were looking for a gunman in Bomber jacket, jeans and Docs, add to this a rough shave and a crew cut and you had the archetypal picture of an IRA gunman. The sad thing was that too many volunteers did dress like this and is it any wonder that they ended up dead or imprisoned at an early age. It was like wearing an IRA uniform and wearing this crap and socialising together was the greatest security Faux Pas you could commit it lead to the direct attrition of volunteers and gave them a one way ticket for Long Kesh.

Myself and Clinger who was doing the driving masked up and went in the back door of the house and caught the family at breakfast, we jumped in and shouted Irish Republican Army how many in the house. There were 3 men and 2 women excluding the parents and I told them to collect in the kitchen they fussed around a little and I and Clinger realised at the same time that there was something wrong. One of the girls was missing along with one of the men and I told Clinger to stay downstairs and watch the rest of the family while I took the stairs two at a time and ran to a bedroom from which the was a lot of noise going on, I found a guy in his underpants trying to climb out the window and a girl screaming at him to hurry up ,his clothes were laying at the foot of the bed and they were a uniform a Royal Navy uniform, I told him to stop and get back in   and   then   pistol   whipped   him   until   he   was   nearly unconscious . He was the eldest girls boyfriend and had been sneaking in to visit her for years. So we settled down to wait for the Japs and it was along wait, the Foot Patrols never arrived until around 6pm that evening by which time we were fed up. All day we had been discussing what to do with the sailor and we still hadn't come up with an answer, Clinger was all for nutting him but I wasn't so convinced that it would be the right thing to do I think in publicity terms we would get a roasting. The family were getting taken to the toilet and one of them overheard us making the decision not to shoot the the asshole but instead to let him live based on the fact that we had never fought the Royal Navy and although they were part of the Security Forces they had never served in N.Ireland and as they say all the nice girls love a sailor. I went and officially informed him of this and he thanked me profusely so I knocked out his two front teeth and told him just how lucky he was and we didn't give a rat's ass for him but just didn't need the bad publicity. The Brits had come down Comedagh Gardens and were standing at the corner off NorthLink. I had opened the back bedroom window and pulled the dressing table in front of it to use as a rifle stand with a pillow underneath it.Clinger was looking like he wanted to say something although I had already guessed that it was based on the fact that he had chosen an M1 Garrand for the job and I knew it was his weapon of choice. I told him to speak up and he blurted out that he would like to take the shot if I was ok with me so I said "knock yourself out but don't fucking miss" I waved to our scout and he cleared of running for a safe house not too far away

I went outside and got the car started and not more than a couple of seconds after that Clinger let loose with a single shot. He came barrelling out the door and threw himself into the car saying" I got him, I got him "so I put the car in gear and we took off, in reverse, Bollox, I said and put it in gear again and we took off again in reverse, for fuck sake Clinger said go will you so I tried again and it was third time lucky. I drove slowly and carefully around Commedagh Hill and down Fruithill Park until we reached the Andytown road where I turned right up the road Road and left down Stockmans Lane and disappeared into safety where we dumped the car up behind a safe house with the Garrand rifle in the boot. Clinger was over the moon about shooting the Brit and was on a real high so I told him about the other part of the job, what other part he said dubiously and I told him about the Booby Trap bomb in the garage so I told him to hold off on the congratulants until we could confirm how the whole operation had gone. It was well after tea time and we were just getting something to eat when we heard the explosion it was a massive bang even though it came from nearly a mile away and I remember thinking oh fuck that sounds awful big for a 15to 20lb bomb. On the news that night it gave out that one Brit had been shot dead and in the follow up search a garage had blown up and seriously injured three soldiers .The following week I saw Twig coming out of the local shops and I said hello but he blanked me" what's wrong with you "I asked him and he told me that the bomb had been so big that it had demolished his Ma's house along with the garage and he was now homeless" thanks for fuck all " were his parting words to me and he never spoke to me again.

CHAPTER 13:

There was no real Sinn Fein in the early 70s or rather there was a Sinn Fein but it was virtually powerless and ineffectual. However we went to see Sinn Fein as it was at that time and somehow they managed to get Twigs family re-housed in a bigger and better house, at that time they could pull and did pull strings to get things done and weren't afraid to muck in. Now days there so politically correct and up their own arseholes that they are afraid to help anyone in case one of their comrades rats them out, so they are whiter than white and about as useful as tits on a bull. They had frequent marches and rally's which they held at the drop of a hat and I enjoyed following along after them because you were nearly always guaranteed a good riot at which you could release your pent up anger by battering Brits around the head with bricks and stones. On day we were picking up an Armalite Rifle from a house in St Agnes Drive and had intended on bringing it up to Lenadoon to be used in a shooting the following day, I had the Butt folded down and was about to go out to the car when I heard the beat of drums and flutes and chanting coming from somewhere up the hill. So I hid the rifle up my jacket and walked to the corner. Coming down the hill from my right hand side was a little Tiocfaidh Band playing Sean South From Garryowen with at least two hundred men, women and children marching along behind them and at the front were at least a half dozen people carrying Banners and right at the front was Marie Drumm . I looked to the left and there were at least fifty Brits with a sprinkling off RUC surrounding the Busy Bee car park the closest of them not more than thirty yards from where I was standing. But all this paled into insignificance when I saw the prizes all standing in a row on the opposite side of the street with their backs to the wall Five senior RUC officers with all the gold Braid and scrambled egg on their hats. I couldn't tell their ranks but I was nearly sure that one of them looked very like Graham Shillington the Chief Constable of the RUC. If ever the phrase between a rock and a hard place was appropriate it surely had to be at this moment. In the space of a few seconds I ran through a myriad of different outcomes which would follow depending on what I decided to do here. The first was to pop around the corner of the house and take out the five senior RUC men, resulting in a few different outcomes the main one being the Brits returning fire up the hill and killing half the marchers on the parade. The next one being the marchers run for cover and the Brits only shoot a few of them. I shoot the five Boyo's and then stay long enough to use up all 30 rounds in the Mag before heroically getting myself blown shitless while trying to escape. You can see were this is going and none of the scenarios are optimal so I did what in the end I knew would have to do and slunk off without firing a shot and the fact that I probably saved numerous lives by running away seemed like a pitiful recompense. Clinger who was driving the car that day didn't understand the decision that I had to make and was totally pissed off that I hadn't taken the shot, Clinger only saw things in black and white anyway and I realised that even representing two dimensional people he still was right when he said that the majority off our operatives would have taken the shot and fuck the Begrudgers , I was thankful for small mercies that it was me on the trigger that day and not him or we might well have had The Andersonstown Massacre.

It wasn't too long after this that we had complacency on our part, one of which was nearly fatal and the other nearly ended up in our capture by the Brits. Just across the road from where the aforementioned shooting never took place was a fairly new set of Garages sitting in a little Cul De Sac off Slievegallion drive one of which we used as an arms dump. There was an old Austin Cambridge parked inside which actually ran but we never used it for driving only for storing weapons. The car itself we kept up on blocks so that anyone looking at it thought it was a wreck what with a flat tyre that we always kept that way and propped up against the side of the car and the bonnet that was always kept up and open to make the car seem as derelict as possible. The fact was it was ready to go in less than 5 minutes at any time. On our way to Ballycastle that day there were four of us in my Volkswagen Beetle two boys and girls heading away for the weekend and mightily looking forward to the break, it's always the same the amount of loose ends you have to tie up just to get away for a bit of R&R and one of those loose ends was what had us at the Garage that summers morning. An ASU in Gransha was going to pull off a job on the Glen Road and they wanted the loan of an Armalite from us, one of the ones that we kept in the Garage they wanted that one in particular because it was fitted with Optics and was point blank accurate and set for 2 hundred yards. In fact I was tempted to say no to these clowns as they had never pulled off a job successfully in their lives but it would have caused hassle over the week end and I would have bet that some spastic would have been sent to our Dump to get the Rifle no matter what I had said. Some people just can't take no for an answer. So we decided to do this last thing before heading off for the weekend, normally we set out a couple of scouts to check the area around a dump before going anywhere near it but this weekend I was thinking with my cock instead of my brain and I decided to take the chance and go in without taking our normal safety precautions. So we arranged to meet the Gransha boys at the Dump at exactly 10/30am and get the loaner done and dusted as the faster we could get finished the faster we could be on our way and let the games commence etc, etc. I heard the roar of a motorbike and the two boys pulled in to the yard we literally threw the Armalite at them and the pillion passenger shoved a bag over it and they disappeared already burning rubber out of the yard, myself and one of the girs went back into the garage for a minute just to put everything back in its place, all that was left in the way of weapons was an RPG 7 and an old .45 colt revolver so we finished choreographing the little scene and we left to lock up the door, but I heard a noise and looked up from scoping my birds ass I saw at least four open back land rovers and around and about twenty Brits all standing in the yard looking menacing, the ass fell out of my world but like a true professional I had a smile on my face as I dandered over to the officer who seemed to be in charge and gave him a good morning as I ushered my bird into the back seat and then I climbed into the front passenger seat and prepared to leave. "Good morning my ass" the officer said" and get fucking out of the car". They searched the Volkswagen and then P Checked the four of us while this was going on I kept looking at my watch and tutting until eventually the officer said are you going somewhere what's with the constant checking the time, I'm sorry about that I don't mind to be rude but I've to be at the Royal Victoria Hospital for eleven o clock to have my ingrowing toe nails removed you know yourself how long it takes to get an appointment to get anything I've been in agony for six months waiting for this operation and I'm nearly late as it is , could you give me a note for the hospital to prove that I was really stopped by the Army and that's why I got held up. The Brits burst out in roars of laughter and one of them shouted to the officer go on Sir give the nonce a note for his mammy. Things noticeably lightened and the brits from my Dads Army attitude stopped perceiving us as a threat and I began to see a glimmer of hope but it was quickly dashed when the Officer told me to open the Lock Up and he walked me in to have a look around. He questioned me as to the ownership of the old car and I told him that it was my previous car before my Da gave me the VW. He put his hand to the glass and tried to look inside but the deep shadow inside the garage made this almost impossible. He asked me what we were doing there and I told him we had called in so my mate could have a quick look at the car as he was thinking of buying it, the doors were all locked and I was told to get the key which I was glad to do as the car had the RPG under it and the inside of the car was totally empty, the Colt .45 was hidden deep inside the engine and covered by a handful of tools that were camouflaging it. Then the officer got me to open the driver's door which left the rest of them still locked and we had disabled them except for the boot because we knew from experience that the Security Forces always insisted on checking it first like it was in the Manual for car searching if there was such an item. He was stuck in the door as he tried to wriggle into the interior of the car which wasn't an easy thing to do wearing a Flack Jacket and carrying a rifle and when he finally managed to extricate himself from the car he was running sweat all down his face and neck. I wondered why he didn't order one of the Squaddies to do it but he just seemed to be a sort of hands on chap. He realised that the Rank and File were having a good laugh behind his back and he made a split second decision to end the situation by telling me to lock up the garage and get in my car along with my companions and fuck off and get my toenails painted or whatever fucking Paddy nonsense I was up to, I tried to stop the relief from showing on my face and the others pretended to look unsurprised at our freedom. Instances like this surely knocked up your acting skill set, increased your ability to lie at the drop of a hat and think on your feet, those that couldn't well they didn't last long. As we headed off on the trip to Ballycastle the car was very subdued there was a rather large elephant in the car with us that we were all trying to ignore finally my birds bad temper got the best of her and she blurted out "that was a fucking set, up if there ever was one" and with that sentiment we all agreed .I said I had no doubt it was a set up but without looking a gift horse in the mouth, why didn't they blow us away. This for a second tossed out the nasty idea that one of us in the car was a tout but I hit that on the head by pointing out the obvious that it would be suicidal as the Brits would have to kill us all, in a shoot to kill like this nearly was you couldn't leave behind any witnesses. There was the two boys on the motor bike but again we agreed they could easily have rolled in at the wrong time and gotten murdered with the rest of us once we had opened this can of worms we realised that the Brits now knew our Car, Make and

Reg where we were going and when we would get there. Everyone was annoyed and pissed off when they realised the trip away for the weekend was off as it was now too dangerous to continue. Until I said "I have a cunning plan" which in actual fact wasn't so cunning, we would just go down south across the Border and Whoop it up in A Border town saloon. Anyway the upshot of all this came to nought because when we got back there were other prioritise and although we told the higher ups the story, I was fairly sure they didn't believe our conclusion's, in the end they long fingered it and let it become someone else's problem only there was no one else.

CHAPTER 14:

The other bad instance we had, happened just a wee while after this and involved myself and our ASU QM a lad nicknamed Curley as his hair was as straight as a dye, he was an excellent QM mainly because he was available morning, noon and night he didn't socialise much and was totally fearless. He was also able to keep in his head the whereabouts of every weapon, in what operational condition it was in and how much ammo there was available for it. At any given time our ASU had two pistols and four or five rifles with assorted ammunition and a variety box of hand grenades nail bombs and self igniting petrol bombs, we didn't have explosives mainly because we hadn't got anyone to make them up for us and anyway it was very difficult to get people to store explosives in their homes. There was one area in which Curly let us down and that was setting the sights on the rifles that we were using for combat. This was a real pain in the hole for me as I had to set the sights on these weapons which was no easy task to achieve in a built up area like Andersonstown so we tended to try and hold onto our weapons and not lend them out to other ASU's because they inevitably came back to us in shite order and I had to re-set them all over again. The other ASU's were aware of the fact that our weapons were always accurate and they often went behind our backs to Batt Staff and tried to force us to lend them and we for our part lied like fuck and constantly claimed that we had nothing to spare as they were all being used on on- going operations.

It was to fix up one of our rifles a Scoped FN that myself and Curley found ourselves one afternoon climbing into the grounds off the Holy Child Primary School. Curley had for sometime been using the school as an arms dump and he had set up a little firing range that was as good as it gets in a built up area constantly patrolled by the enemy where a gunshot can bring the Security Forces down on top of you in minutes. Our set up was like this ,there were temporary wooden classrooms placed all around the school yards which were set around five feet high on stilts presumably to keep the bottom of them dry and rubbish free. A six step set of stairs led to a double door and the platform was just level with it. The huts themselves were around twenty feet wide by thirty feet long and had windows along both sides and most importantly they had an attic to which the only access was a two foot square trap door built into the roof of a little storeroom that was partitioned off from the rest of the classroom. The particular hut that we had picked stood on its own in a tiny little yard squashed between a small Tarmac pathway on one side and a ten foot high grass bank on the other side which made a v shape as the grassy bank sloped away from the classroom wall. The weapons to be fixed were brought by Curley and hidden in the attic a few days before I went in to set them. Also we had cut a little hole just big enough to shoot through which overlooked a wall of the school boiler room which coincidentally had large signs which were almost exactly two hundred yards from the firing point. This was our set up and it worked well an added bonus was that when you fired from further back in the attic the noise of the shot was dramatically lessened by the structure of the building which was fairly well soundproofed. So we proceeded as we had ten times previously we gained access through a window with a latch slightly damaged which could be prised open from the outside and once in we went into the store room and pulled a table under the attic hatch and helped each other up and into the roof space. The guns were hidden in a hollow between the wall of the building and the lowest edge of the roof with a plank fitted over the top to keep them covered. As I was setting every gun to the same distance 150 yds. which for most of them is point blank range I tried to lessen the danger of the firing being audible by firing a maximum of five shots with which to set them as accurately as possible? Off course all off this fuckology would have been a lot less necessary if the pricks that were borrowing the weapons didn't screw around with them I even got to the stage were when I was finished setting a set of scopes I taped up the adjustment dials in the hope it would discourage any budding artificers from fiddling with them. So I got to business with the rifle and to be perfectly honest I found the sights were not too far off as my first shot hit within an inch or two of the target I fired again just to check and I hit almost in the same spot so I reckoned that'll do ,yes that'll do nicely. I gave the weapon to Curley and he squirreled it away in the eve of the roof and he had just finished when I heard the crackling chatter of a Brit two way radio coming from outside. I hissed to Curley and made a shushing motion with my finger to my lips to indicate that we had company and needed to be quiet. I listened closer but it was hard to hear anything above the frantic beating off my own heart. There was noise all around us now foot treads up and down the steps, the rattle of the lock.

All off a sudden there was the roar of a Brit voice shouting" We know you're in there come to the front door open it up and step outside, I promise you will be in no trouble ". No trouble my arse, we were hanging and it didn't look too chipper from our side. Myself and Curley crawled to the side of the wall closest to the grassy bank and lay there on the floor tight to the bottom of the wall. The Brits by this time had sent some men to our side and were shining flash lamps through the windows. Then they began to pound on the walls an attempt to see in and they were threatening to shoot through the walls. Then they went to the top of the steps and attempted to kick the front door in, but it was holding firm .I called Curley closer and whispered in his ear that we would have to make a move or they would eventually get us. So we slipped along the bottom of the wall and just when we had gotten below the window I felt Curley tense up and stop moving. I whispered what's wrong and I looked in front of him in front of him and there was a spider the size of your thumb. I would have liked to have squashed him but instead had to make do with Mr Spider, making a miraculous escape I hoped it was a good sign for us. It was time to go and we went to our egress point and literally slithered out the window and dropped noiselessly to the bottom of the grassy bank as bad luck would have it we dropped right on top off a Brit who was standing having a piss against the wall of the cabin , myself and curly tried to subdue him but he was a strong bastard and whilst we had our hands clamped to his mouth he was starting to wriggle free I started to laugh and both Curley and the Brit froze and looked at me like I was fuckin nuts as I thought if the Brit survived this he would be known to his mates as Wriggle Free. It's a funny old world aint it and to make it even more ridiculous Curley hissed to me that he had a gun with him, this news made the brit redouble his effortrs to escape and Curley was beginning to loose his grip on him .He said it's in my pocket take it which I did in a flash and had it pressed against his forehead. He knew that if we shot him his mates were only a few feet away and any second they would step around the corner of the cabin and our goose was cooked but I wasn't called ==== for nothing and I had a cunning plan. Luckily the gun was a .38 Smith & Wesson Revolver and I cocked it and held it to his head and calmly informed him that if his mates opened fire my dead thumb would release the pressure on the hammer. We held him in front of us like a shield Just on que the Brits appeared and he screamed at his mates not to shoot and pointed out the situation he was in. It had gotten dark by this time and I said calmly to the Brits "were going to back away and if any of you shoot or follow us I'll blow this bastards head off". The trick is not to give them time to think but to keep everything moving right along. The Brits were raging and any second I expected to hear and feel the bullets striking me but we had backed down a large flight of stone steps and were half way across the school yard. I didn't want to shoot him because that would have provoked an immediate reaction from the brits instead we just turned and disappeared into the darkness and to the accompaniment of bursts of gunfire we legged it to the fence and dived over it. It's hard to shoot in the dark especially when your targets are zig zagging and running for their lives. We ran down Coram Ring(didn't see Pa Bear or the white horse) and went into the Ex-servicemen's club. We looked a bit rough; a bullet had flashed right past my eye and it was watering like fuck and wouldn't stop and I was more concerned that people would think that I was crying also there was a scorch mark on my balls were another bullet had ripped a hole in my crotch. Curley was reasonably ok except he had, had the heels blown of his shoes but one of the lads assured him that there were a couple of stiffs in the keg store and he could have his pick of their shoes. If you have ever hidden in the dark and your life depended on it you will never want to repeat the experience. It's only then that you realise how good your hearing is and how you can hear little sounds that you've never heard before even little internal noises like your belly rumbling your heart beating and the sound of your breathing. I told Curley to go home and get some sleep time and I took my own advice and did the same. The following day I called down to see him to see if anything could be salvaged from the debacle of the previous night and found him with a smile from ear to ear like the Cheshire cat as he informed me that himself and two of his little Fianna helpers had gone back into the school and rescued the rifle so the Brits would never know that we were using it as a dump. I was gobsmacked at the nieveatie of the lad and the fact that he didn't understand just how lucky he and the two other two munchkins were to be alive. My intention had been to set up an ambush at the school and when the Brits came to set up their ambush we would be in first and waiting for them. It was my acessemnt that the Brits had found the Gun and would set the SAS to cover it and kill whoever came to pick it up. The only thing the Brits had done wrong was they had taken too long to get the murder squad in place. Well I read the Riot Act and pointed out that they had acted with total stupidity and how insane it was to have done what they did but I could see in their eyes that they weren't taking all of this in and Curley said that they felt deeply fuckin unappreciated and sloped off licking their bruised egos.

CHAPTER 15:

We set up a sting operation as the Brits obviously didn't know that the three Musketeers Asshole, Pathetic and Inept had been there and already robbed the cookie jar. It took two days to spot the Brit ambush there were two of them set up on a section of the school roof which overlooked the temporary classroom and we couldn't get a shot at them, we would have made too much noise in trying to get up the last downpipe to get level with the flat roof so we improvised. I sent a little squad off young kids around to the Cabin with a rubber ball and told them to start a game of handball. This hopefully attracted the attention of the two SAS on the roof while I and Clinger lobbed three hand grenades up onto the flat roof. The Brits had nowhere to hide and the three explosions killed them both in fact one of them was blown right off the roof and landed in a bloody heap fifty feet below where the Handball squad gratefully stripped him of his rifle and pistol which were attached to his body. Again I would like to make it clear that when dealing with the kids from the Fianna or indeed anyone else for that matter orders and instructions were always passed along by a third party at least in my ASU I was aware of others who weren't as security conscious and the result was they were swelling the ranks in Long Kesh at an alarming rate. I'm not saying that the internees in Long Kesh were all careless far from it we all took our lives and our freedom very seriously but there was no if you got Interned, it was only a matter of when and how long you could evade the inevitable. The kids were a help and a hindrance as well they were good in gaining low level intelligence they went everywhere and saw everything. They followed foot patrols about the streets and they watched for patterns like were the Brits stopped to piss were they stopped and had a sandwich were they took a sly five minute break and of course who were the Brits speaking to on their patrols and more importantly who was speaking to them. Un- fortunately there was some serious down sides to using them the little fuckers were watching us just as intently and given that they were kids they were easily broken when taken in for interrogation by the Brits. When it was discovered by our own intelligence core that this or that kid had broken we forced them to leave the country for a while or to go and stay with relatives until they were allowed back. One of the most shameful episodes I can recall was two teenagers Bugsy Mc Crory and Bru Mc Kinney who were both disappeared and executed and their bodies not returned to their family's for many years.

At that time in 1972 the Brits didn't realise how much of an asset the Fianna and the Camman na mBan really were or they would have targeted them mercilessly but they were mostly a male chauvinist organisation and they lived with the stereotype of the denim clad skinhead in the cities and the big hairy farmer in the countryside. When in reality we were handsome and dashing types like John Wayne, Errol Flynn and Lon Chaney who could howl with the best of us. Yea and if your Granny had balls she'd be your Granda. Whereas we had no misconceptions about our enemies we knew what the British Army was and what it was prepared to do to win, like the roll the SAS played which has been overrated in the context of the war as a whole they hid and operated from behind your average squaddie and ran very little risk to themselves as most of the volunteers they murdered were set up and unarmed. Then there was the RUC who just simply needed put down and last and definitely least the Loyalist paramilitaries who preferred their victims tied up and helpless. Well that's all I have to say about that.

Besides operating almost autonomously we had to be able to react immediately when called upon by Batt or Brigade Staff who usually only got in touch with us when something had gone assways and they wanted us to turn out ready for battle. I was just in from work one evening and my Ma was putting my dinner out when one of the Girls in the ASU came to see me and I knew from the look on her face that I was about to hear something that I would rather not. So I pushed my dinner aside and told her to go ahead and give me the bad news as it was obvious that was what it was. I told her to give me the worst news first and she said I'm sorry but it's all worst news. Two of our volunteers were planting a bomb in a Nightclub down town and the job went wrong and it seems that one of them was shot and killed he was from Turf Lodge and the other one was a girl and she was shot and seriously injured that's all we know at the moment but Batt Staff says your to get everybody out and armed right now and go to her house and tie in with any other ASU's on the scene because as soon as the Brits get her name they 'll raid the house and were going to or rather you're going to ambush them.

My ma had overheard as she always did and she said as I was grabbing my coat what will I do with this good dinner , do you want to take the bit of steak to eat on your way so I told her kindly to put it in the oven or preferably the dog. Don't worry she said it'll be here when you get back.

When we arrived at the Volunteers house the street was empty but the streets surrounding it were a hive of activity one house was being used as a dump and there was a box van offloading a small arsenal into it so we headed in and picked what ever weapons we could the choice was simple it was AR180's or AR180's I was happy enough with that the Armalites were new and undamaged and factory set and there was loads off spare mags all loaded and ready for action. Somebody has been really busy I said to the lads it's good to see a bit of organisation for a change. Altogether I counted about 30 shooters all moving into positions and Myself and a couple of more experienced heads went around checking the field of fire making sure there were no crossfires or heroes too close in and in the line of fire. All the time there were volunteers knocking on houses up and down the street telling people to get into their back upstairs bedrooms and to pull furniture and mattresses around them and just in case pulling out the phones from the few houses that had one just in case someone was tempted to call 999.Some people moved out altogether and quickly moved in with friends or relatives in adjoining streets. It was definitely going to be a protracted fire fight and we set up a few ambush sites who had our backs in the eventuality that the Brits having vastly superior numbers and firepower would eventually flank us. If that took place then we wanted as much time as possible to bug out. As soon as we were ready we reminded everyone that it was our people in the firing line and not to be shooting into houses only if absolutely necessary and even then only at downstairs targets. The fact was we were using civilians as shields to ham string the Brits so that they couldn't bring heavy weapons to bear on our positions and they used civillians as cover by patrolling in the midst of them and to hide behind when they came under fire and both sides were ready with the propaganda and spin in the eventuality that anything fucked up, we were all cavalier with other people's lives and I never met one of us from either side that suffered from PTSD who wasn't a big girls blouse.

A Saracen , a Pig and a Whippet have a very distinctive engine whine and you can recognise enemy vehicles from a mile away particularly at night time when just the sound of them can tighten your sphincter mussels, the same as a two way radio when you hear it ahead of you or even an English accent . In this case it was the whine of the army vehicles that put us all on ready , steady was when they had taken up position and go was to be the first shot fired by our Commander. In they came like Noah's Ark two by two, two Saracens, two Pigs and two jeeps about 30 squaddies in all discounting the vehicle crews of about 10 which was a total of circa 40. They wasted no time in disembarking and took up positions at about fifty yards either side of the house. It's amazing how quickly people can adapt in a situation like this, one moment their sitting in their cosy living rooms watching the news and the war on TV in a heartbeat they are the on the news and in the war. This is where being part of a community is all important.

It's the moral high ground when people say to you it's all right for you putting some other poor sods in danger and you can tell them, yeah some of the poor sods you're talking about are my family who are in the houses down there on the firing line. By this time it was getting dark and the Brits had taken up their covering positions when our commander gave the go signal when he opened fire and over 30 weapons fired a split second later. There was pandemonium among the Brits as they flung themselves into any cover they could find and they had a half dozen men hit in the first volley and we were so close a couple of them threw themselves into cover on top of us and we stiffed them immediately. One of them was shouting orders obviously an Officer or NCO and I shut him up with a bullet to the head which dropped him where he stood and left him writhing around on the road with his nervous system refusing to shut down. The Brits returned fire in a ragged volley but it was clear we were getting the best of them and even in the first minute it was clear that they had no answer to our firepower, some of them jumped into a Saracen and slammed the door closed and returned fire through the viewing ports and one of them opened up with a Browning 30 cal machine gun which had the potential to cut us to pieces when into the breech stepped Curley with an RPG and gave it one up the arse which turned the crew into soup. The Brits realised that things were looking black around the coal quays for them and they did what we hoped they wouldn't but knew they would they smashed the windows of the houses in and opened the doors taking cover in the houses. This made it much more difficult for us and slowed our return fire down considerably. They also discovered the family's taking cover upstairs and some off them used this to their obvious advantage when they realised that we weren't returning fire to the upstairs of the houses. We had told everyone to switch on their ground floor lights which gave us good target acquisition for a while at least until the Brits realised this and turned them off. Also we soon found that they were using blind fire when returning fire at us and it made us much more confident as the fire fight roared on. All the nonsense that some shooters give you about the noise a bullet makes when it goes by your head is just that nonsense with the noise of the rifle fire and the sound of exploding masonry and bricks you can barely hear yourself think never mind hearing bullets supposedly whizzing past your head. We had a couple of hand grenades but couldn't use them for fear of killing or wounding people in the houses the same applied to our RPG we couldn't use that against the houses either for the same reason. The Brits on the other hand didn't have their Mothers, Fathers, and Brothers, Sisters or children in the houses and had no restraint in firing back. This left us in a position of diminishing returns we were now engaging the Brits in a shot for shot gun battle and getting no real results from it plus the fact that the Brits were trying to flank us from the Glen Road and we had lost a couple of volunteers one of whom was a female volunteer who had been shot in the head we decided to call it quits and disappear, the final action of the night was left to Curley who put a farewell rocket up the arse of the other Saracen armoured car just as a parting gift. In five minutes we were all gone and all that was left were piles of empty bullet casings broken glass and a lot of pockmarked houses were bullets had left their signature. The Brits came in convoys after this and raided houses all over the estate and collected most of the empty bullet casings and washed the blood away from anywhere they found it. Needless to say they were no happy bunnies and lots of gratuitous beatings and violence was rained down on the local population for the whole of the next day until the Brits felt that they had satisfied their need for revenge. They found one young volunteer out moving a rifle from one dump to another for which there was no need and he was lucky not to have been shot, instead they made him lie down against the footpath and proceeded to jump up and down on his arms and legs until they had broken all four of them. He later got 15 years in Crumlin road Gaol for his stupidity and walked with a limp for the rest of his life and was forever known as Hopalong although his second name wasn't Cassidy. If it had been he'd have been called Butch a result of watching too manty westerns on TV when we were kids.

A couple of days later we got the sceal on what had happened at the Celebrity club, a neighbour of mine had been planting a bomb at the club and the operation had gone ass ways when the car pulled up outside and two of the Bomb team jumped out carrying the bomb in a holdall and brandishing pistols. They shouted Provisional IRA we are planting a bomb here and it has an anti-handling device attached if you attempt to move it, it will explode right away, you have 10 minutes to get out of the building and with that done they legged it back to the car but as they climbed in the driver looking in the rear view mirror could not see any activity. So the bomb team ran back to the club again brandishing their pistols and again shouting a warning, however this time they noticed that the doorman was totally pissed and was too drunk to understand what was going down. They clubbed him around the head in hopes of waking him up but there was no joy, so they ran through the foyer until they met a small group of people standing just inside the doors and they relayed the bomb warning to them and then ran back out to the car. Again nothing happened and their time was running out the bomb wasn't supposed to kill anyone it was meant to destroy property this time when they ran back to the club they intended on taking the bomb somewhere else and dumping it. An always an anyways as they ran into the club it was too late and they met a crowd of people screaming and running out. In the vanguard of the crowd were undercover RUC men who happened to be in there on a night out and spotting the two volunteers with handguns, opened fire and killed one volunteer Martin Forsythe and shot the other one a female volunteer who was hit at the top of the spine and was paralyzed from the chest down. She went on to get married have children and lead a successful life although she was severely handicapped for the remainder of her days.

My mother and father who had been trapped in their house during the gun battle along with my brothers and sisters told me some of what had taken place in the house. The Brits had smashed in the front windows and dived through into the house intent on using it as cover. She said that just a minute or two later another three soldiers had come flying in the windows to make the total eight of them hiding in the house. She was upstairs at the time and heard a ruckus and commotion going on downstairs. She shouted that she was coming down stairs and not to be bloody shooting her and when she got there she found two Brits obviously officers who had two young squaddies by the neck and were trying to throw them out the back door and into the garden were the fighting was intense and in fact was hand to hand in some instances. The young squaddies were struggling and holding onto kitchen furniture and refusing sensibly to go out there. My ma doing what women of that age always seem to do put the teapot on and made tea and gave Chocolate Digestives to everybody when they were eating they weren't shooting at our kids. She rounded on the officers and told them they should be ashamed of themselves treating little youngsters that way. So she called three of the youngest Brits over and hugged them and told them everything would be alright. They sat there the rest of the time and never fired a shot and the Officer who had completely lost his temper by this time left the room and never came back. So much for the so called training and discipline of the British Army my Ma could have bate them all with an oul slipper. This gun battle was never reported on TV and it was like the hundreds of other incidents that took place the Brits liked to keep the Ministry of Misinformation well stocked and they didn't like the public particularly the British public to know the extent of the war in N Ireland and as for us they didn't give a shite about what we knew or didn't know , our opinions were just so much wasted air. The Corporation Housing Authority turned up a couple of days later and fixed up all the damage so that there was no evidence left to show that anything had taken place at all. Also there was the usual spate of bus crashes in Germany and other areas were the BA could claim uncheckable accidents. The order of the day seemed to be if it was deniable deny it . I sometimes wondered what their families would think when their son who was serving in N Ireland supposedly ended up dead in a parachute accident in the highlands of Scotland , especially since he wasn't a paratrooper. It would be a hard sell to convince the Great British unwashed that this was a police action.

A month flew by and it was a lot of same o, same o. I tried to go to work as often as I could to hold down a job I Didn't give a shit about , not that it was a bad job in fact most people would have given their right arm for it , sixty pounds a week was the salary which in 1972 /73 was great money and It was virtually impossible to get sacked short of committing murder (no pun intended). We were all really jaded and the weather was hot and it was hard to drum up any enthusiasm for anything that required a lot of effort so we fell back on our old reliable shoot and scoot. However when you start taking things for granted and you stop paying attention to detail that's the time you pay the piper for complacency.

CHAPTER 16:

It was in these areas that you found Peelers driving around in Jeeps and cars with no back up also the Brits were inclined to frequent these areas in open topped jeeps and the whole lot of them Peelers and Brits alike went into the local Protestant shops for Cigarettes and groceries and stuff. All you had to do was to get a jeep or car on its own somewhere and get in close and shoot em up. Obviously there are some sweet spots that the security forces frequented more often than others and we found that we could hit these with regularity and by the time the Brits in particular had copped on to them their tour of duty was up and the new regiment coming in were starting from scratch. However the Security forces were catching on while we were growing complacent and the combination of the two was bound in the end to lead to a bad outcome and so it did. One of these sweet spots was the bottom off Blacks Road where it meets the Lisburn Road a good place for us as we had gotten a Brit and two Peelers there, so on a lovely summer evening we ventured down in the hopes of repeating our success. Clinger was driving the car and I was in the passenger seat holding a Armalite rifle with the butt folded down we had driven past the Kells Avenue Estate and there were a couple of Orange gangs knocking about and we were happy that if there was no go on the Lisburn Road that we would do a drive by on the Orange men as we came back up. As it turned out there was a Peeler jeep parked near the bridge and it looked like they were stopping for Tax and insurance. This will do I told Clinger and he pulled the car smoothly into the side of the road about fifty yards from the road block. I climbed out with the Armalite cocked and ready to go and took a firing position over the roof of the car. The Aramlite had a two power scope on it and I sighted in on the head of one of the peelers when the world turned to shite and a dozen or more bullets hit the car all around me it wasn't the peelers at the road block that opened fir it seemed to be coming from off to the side of me. I returned fire but the shooting got worse and I heard Clinger moan as one of the bullets hit him I shouted at him to swing the car around and as he began to do a u turn on the road I walked beside the car firing at where I could see the shooting coming from and I kept walking and firing until Clinger got the car turned but just before I could jump in I felt a blow to my side and I knew I had been hit, there was no pain but as I climbed into the car I felt blood running down my side and Clinger was no better he had got shot through the ass and blood was starting to pool on his driver's seat. While Clinger got the car the hell out of there I changed Mags and kept returning fire as all the while the car sounded like it was being hit by a shower of hailstones. After getting back to Andytown we dumped the car which looked like a sieve and made our way to a safe house where the people in the house could get us medical attention and see how bad the wounds were. Mine weren't too bad as I had been hit by a 9mm round which entered my side and lodged there not too far into my flesh, it must have come through the body of the car which luckily for me took much of the sting out of it. Unfortunately for Clinger his wound became infected and it got to the stage that the Republican medical team who gave us minor medical repairs couldn't cope anymore and we smuggled him across the border to Our Lady of Lourdes Hospital in Drogheda and we didn't see him again for nearly six months. The infection spread to his Bowel and he almost didn't make it. This shocked me first because it made me realise that I wasn't invulnerable and second we only thought in terms of capture, escape or death we never gave a thought about being wounded so badly that the remainder of your life was lived in pain and suffering. Any who the fact that the Brits reached out and touched us was disconcerting to say the least and it made me just a tad annoyed so we wanted blood for this but at the same time I wasn't feeling too chipper so I called the girls and we worked out the sort of a plan that shouldn't work but that is so audacious and complicated in its conception than when it does work sends shockwaves of disgust through the general public. This sort of operation was right down the girl's alley and they sat about it with gusto. The first thing we needed was a stage on which to paint our masterpiece and we settled for the railings alongside the Christin Brothers Secondary School on the Glen road. The next order of business was to get a bomb made up with a Mercury Tilt Switch on it so that when it was set and primed it couldn't be moved or it would detonate and then we had to find a Manikin which was no easy job I can tell you but we finally located one at a closed down Tailors shop in Castle Street. The storeman who looked after it tried to black mail the girls into having to buy the fuckin thing but three of them made him lie down and took his driving licence and in no uncertain terms told him that the use of the Manikin could not be traced back to him and if he said anything to anyone we would shoot his whole worthless little family. The manikin was of a young girl and the Girls made it up to perfection. The next item on our shopping list was animal blood only blood looks and smells like blood we went to the local butchers and got three litres of it. All this preparation was taking a while and the girls were starting to lose faith and the will to live the longer it went on. I expressed my doubts to one of them and she took me to bed and afterward I felt a lot better. The other girls didn't know about the odd shags I got from her and another girl but we were all very young and sometimes the urge grew so insistent, that we couldn't help ourselves anyway and always we treated each other with respect and eventually I came to realise that I had strong feelings for the two of them and I decided to ask one of them out when I got the chance. The two of them were class acts and had more balls than most men I knew. There was no job they wouldn't do and no risk they wouldn't take, the success I had in A Coy was due in no small part to them and although I operated all over Belfast and Antrim and occasionly in Tyrone or south Armagh I never worked with anybody better.

The day of our big plan dawned and the girls were all excited and I was nervous that the job would work and not leave me looking like a Stumer. So we borrowed a car for the job we didn't need to hijack one as the car wouldn't be seen and we could dirty up the number plates. Meanwhile back at the ranch the EO was putting the final touches to the bomb and he was as happy as a pig in shite as he didn't often get to make a bomb with any finesse and he had more booby trap devices on this bomb that it needed and couldn't be diffused once primed it would go bang no matter what happened. He then placed the device into the chest cavity of the manikin and the girls dressed her beautifully and then wrecked her clothes and pulled and hauled her about until she looked like she had taken a beating.

CHAPTER 17:

I drove the car as none of the girls could drive but they sat in the back with the Manikin until we reached our destination which was the CBS School we timed the job to happen late evening so there would be no bystanders and the Brits wouldn't see anything except what we wanted them to. So I pulled the car up and the girls jumped out and pulled the Manikin out with them and chained it to the railings .Then one of them poured blood all over Its legs and then we revved up and fucked off. We pulled the car up into the car park of Bass Charrington and left it there totally clean and walked down to the front of the reception area were we could see the Manikin chained to the railings on the far side of the road we had left a couple of younger girls to stand watch in case on lookers gathered at the scene to make sure that no by standers touched the Body. They were to warn people off from touching the Manikin by saying things like said things like don't touch her and I'd suggest we all get back to a safe distance because the Brits are on the way. The two younger girls had a gun with them just in case some hero decided to mess about with the Manikin before the Brits came. However it turned out that this precaution was unnecessary as the Brits were based in Fort Monagh which was only five minutes away and they got there in record time. Up the road came a Red Cross Saracen armoured car which pulled up beside the unfortunate victim and out jumped two Brit Medics who ran to the scene and began to treat the victim it was their last act of kindness on this earth as there was a small explosion and the two Brits were blown about ten feet up the road with heads and limbs rolling about the road. Again there was more screaming from the assembled on lookers as the concussion from the explosion even though it was only a small bomb blew some of them off their feet. It was later given out that one of the Brits was a Doctor which made the victory that much sweeter as the higher the rank of the victims you can get gives the incident that much more human interest than if it's just another Squaddie who bites the dust.

It was around about this particular period when I met a girl that I really fancied and I began to spend as much time with her as I could in fact when I say I spent a lot of time with her I mean all my waking hours. She was the most beautiful and desirable woman in the world for a guy who practiced the three F's (Find them, Fuck them and Forget about them) had been getting along famously without a regular squeeze I fell like Icarus. She was in the RA of course all of my friends and acquaintances were but that didn't matter I just wanted to be near her. I became jealous of her spending time away from me and in particular with other volunteers doing other jobs. The Brits didn't know what hit them or rather didn't hit them as I stopped operating and there went the most prolific Killer that the RA had at the time. The Brits obviously had no idea that this peaceful reprieve was all down to love and sex. Especially sex. I shagged her everywhere in call houses, in my house, in her house, in cars, up entries everywhere I could think off. The Batt Staff were getting pissed off with me as the shootings in the Andytown area had dropped to almost zero and they sent for me to come down and have a chat with them about the "Hole" situation and I was told in no uncertain terms to keep my Dick in my pants and concentrate on business. Funny enough the Brits were the cause of their own misfortune as they tried to kill me and my girlfriend outside the house. My mother's niece was coming up from the Markets to see her and to introduce her new fiancé to whom she had just gotten engaged. They came down the garden path and down two steps which led to the front door when a car pulled up in front of the house and someone pushed a MP3A1 Grease gun out of the rear passenger window and opened fire on them. They were grazed and shook up but basically unhurt as they dived behind the steps for cover. This incident resulted in a number of things, first the poor girl never came to our house again, secondly she got rid of the Fiancé who left her lying there and legged it down the entry to safety and lastly It pushed me back into the war as I realised that the Brits thought they were shooting at me and my girlfriend. So I backed off on the whole girlfriend thing and she got tired of being long fingered figuratively speaking and left me to my own devices which basically meant that I went back to Girl 1 and Girl 2 for the odd ride. Ah well in the land of the Blind the one eyed milk man is king.

CHAPTER 18:

So I got back to the war and found that the rest of the crew had slacked off and everybody was doing their own thing. In Clinger's absence I got Curley to take over his duties which basically meant backing me up on operations were I needed a second shooter and Curley appointed his next in command to take over as ASU Quarter Master it wasn't the ideal situation as Curley couldn't drive which made things a bit awkward because I often had to bring in a third person to do the driving which was putting another life at risk for no good reason. The new driver was called Spud and he came from the St Merrill part of Andytown an area that we had neglected because of its small size and the fact that there were only two ways in and out of it.

I have always hated confined spaces I wouldn't say that I was claustrophobic but I wouldn't be far off. It's not just small spaces I dislike it any area that is or seems to me to be too small for its purpose. Like for instance Croke park is an ok space but not on all Ireland final day when there are over 80000 people jammed into it or being in a crowded lift with only a few other people in there with me. It's the way I felt about St Merrill and the little estate in lower Andytown I'm sure it was a perfectly good housing estate but the lack of egress gave me a confined feeling and I didn't want to operate in there. Once you fired a shot in this area there was no getting out and you had to stay put in one of the houses and wait to see if the Brits were going to raid the area or not I suppose that depended on how successful your operation had been. We had a few volunteers in the area and even they knew that it was an operational nightmare to work there. There was one major plus that it did have because nothing ever took place there the residents were willing to store Guns, Ammo and Explosives in actual fact it was an excellent place to have as a munitions dump. However it was even better to stage ambushes from as it was bordered on three sides by main roads The Glen Road, The Andytown Road and Kennedy Way. Also the volume of Brit Military traffic was constant due to the fact that there were three major forts being kept supplied along these arterial routes. And right in the middle of all of this activity sat Lower Andytown as a little oasis of peace but not for much longer. The local ASU were over the moon about this and were champing at the bit to get started. All we needed to have on any job in this new area was a rifle and an RPG. There was no point in taking a car in there as you wouldn't get it out again so it was safer to have a safe house that could be used to hide the team. The local ASU leader was only a kid but he seemed mature for his age. The age range of the lads was from seventeen down to fifteen and they were very inexperienced so we decided to give them as much training as we could so we gave them a week on Urban Guerrilla Warfare tactics and a hit that was easy to do and would involve the whole ASU so as to give them some on the ground training. There was a great selection of weapons available and I chose two G3's for myself and Curley and 2 M1 Carbines for two of the lads in the ASU, I decided against using an RPG this first time out for the lads as I didn't want to over complicate their first job. I spent a lot of time with the lads huddled around a kitchen table with little Dinky toys showing them who was going to shoot what and depending on the speed of the convoy how much they would need to lead the targets off and take their time over their shots and not to be emptying magazines as fast as they could pull the trigger. As Michael Collins said "There's to be no riddling". No one had bothered with them before and they were very appreciative of the training. As far as I was concerned I was happy to give them whatever training I could as it would help to extend their survival time by weeks if not months but I knew that would be all they would get as they just didn't know enough and the survival time off an ASU member in 1972 and

1973 was approx. two months before being Killed or Captured.

The rest of the day we spent getting into position and ready to fight and I knew by the sheer volume of Brit traffic on the road that it wouldn't be long before a target would present itself. In actual fact it took less than fifteen minutes for a mobile patrol to come down Monagh Road through the roundabout and down Kennedy Way toward our ambush position we heard them before we saw them and we moved swiftly to our firing positions at the front of the houses overlooking the road and we could see an open back jeep and two lorries coming down the road .It was straight forward shooting and I aimed for the cab of the first lorry and shot through the driver's window and popped him and the shotgun passenger, simultaneously Curley took care of the second lorry as he raked it from stem to stern including the canvas back in case there were any soldiers travelling inside. The other two lads played their part and gave the jeep fifteen rounds apiece out of their M1 Carbines. The result was that the first lorry swerved across the road and the second crashed into it while the jeep although hit a number of times disappeared on down Kennedy Way toward the Andersonstown roundabout. Our runback was short and safe and the whole job went off without a hitch for which I was glad but it was too easy and my sense off anti-climax was there again as my need for danger wasn't satisfied.Also the lads were understandably cock a hoop and I did'nt want to rain on their parade but the job went off to easily and and I did'nt want them to think that all combat was this simple. The graveyards are full of people who were brimming with over confidence.

CHAPTER 19:

I think it was Ernest Hemmingway that said "There is no hunting like the hunting of man and those who have hunted armed men long enough and liked it never care for anything else thereafter". I have found this to be true and those of us, who were successful over the years at playing the great game, all had the same thing in common we were danger junkies who enjoyed playing by big boy's rules. Often people will continuously do things that are not the accepted norm and they wring their hands and say Mea Culpa Mea Maxima Culpa, subscribing to the belief that when you do something that society sees as terrible that you should apologise for it or else people will point at you with disdain and loathing. The world needs a certain amount of Psychopath's and Sociopaths God bless them how could you fight a war without them. I had already decided to do another job soonest as the last one was to easy and I would use an RPG this time to try and up the body count, at the end of the day it was all about the number of body bags that you filled with the opposition's troops and who would blink first. You could bet your sweet patooty that it wouldn't be us.

The News the next morning featured the ambush which wasn't too surprising given the ferocity of the attack and the fact that the main road was blocked. According to them one Brit had been shot and killed and two more had been seriously injured when the trucks had collided and overturned on the road. They didn't bother to raid in the estate realising it was hopeless and the perpetrators would be long gone merging back into the community and into their daily roles as Butcher, Baker and

Candlestick maker. That isn't to say that there would be no retaliation forthcoming, sure as shit some poor bastard would cop as a result of this but it wouldn't be this day. No this day we were satisfied with a job well done and we had already moved on looking for our next go on the road to perdition. The St Merrill Babes as we called them sadly didn't make it more than nine weeks but were caught in an ambush and one died later from Gun Shot Wounds and the ASU commander was arrested at a firearms dump and after getting a ferocious hiding by the Brits he was sentenced to life in Prison and served around 27 years, that is a sad result, I believe when he got out he was still wearing High Waist band flared trousers and Bay City Roller tops and didn't realise that he was now a middle aged man. He missed his whole life the 70s and free love the girls now ready willing and able to drop their kecks at a seconds notice and the old fashioned values gradually drifting away. The church becoming irrelevant and not having the power it once had, I think the fact that I was prepared to shoot a priest as I stated earlier really sums it all up. I was sitting in the Glen Owen Pub one night with my brother when your man the lad that had done the all the time in the Maze came in and I didn't recognise him and my brother whispered to me who he was and before I could stop him my brother invited him over and introduced him to me.

Well what the fuck are you supposed to say to someone like that, there is no small talk that you can make to him? Some one that has served 28 years someone that has been on the dirty protest and gone through the hunger strikes it doesn't bare thinking about. Especially as I was the asshole that trained him up and put him in harm's way. I definitely could feel the presence of the elephant in the corner. To my surprise he genuinely liked me and was over awed by my exploits in battle, he sat with me for hours and recounted the operations I was involved in as though he was there himself I asked him how he knew all this and he said that he followed my involvement in the war through his sisters who were in the Cumman na mBan and got all the gossip on me and gave him all the sceal at his weekly visits, he sort of lived his life through me which helped him to put in his time. I was embarrassed and ashamed that I had used him when he was young and vulnerable until my brother pointed out later that we were all young used and vulnerable, that's just the nature of war. I never saw him again and my brother told me years later that he had died at an early age from stomach cancer. The amount of people I know who have died from cancers and neurological diseases in N Ireland is unbelievable it makes you wonder if the Brits were poisoning us steadily over the years either in some covert fashion or accidently in their attempts to introduce and use new technologies for combatting terrorist groups around the world. Were the Brits who used and tested these things ever checked properly for health problems and are they themselves victims of Black Ops technology. That is only what may have taken place in the Public Domaine it makes you wonder what was done to the Republican prisoners over the years they were held incarcerated in British Gaols.

CHAPTER 20:

A message came to us from Battalion that the IRA Army Council were in the process of having talks with the British Government and they wanted to be in a position of strength while they were doing it. They told us in Andytown that they needed us to up the rate of attacks and scores and told us to get the finger out.

Andytown was by far the main area for upping the casualty rate and we went on a Blitz over a couple of months. The amount of hits we achieved was staggering and the Brits were reeling in shock and wondering where the fuck this had come from.

In one street alone over a two month period we ambushed and hit four Brits, one alongside the wooden fence at the junction of Kenard Avenue and Tullymore Gardens I hit him with a jungle .303 with a single shot to the chest, another one I hit was standing at the door of the Flats half way up Tullymore Gardens two more I hit at the top of Tullymore Gardens at the side of Rossnareen Flats I hit them with an Armalite Rifle at point blank range as they walked toward me and asked me for my I.D. I dropped to one knee less than 15 feet from them and sprayed them with about a dozen rounds. Another one I got was standing at the side wall of a house across the road from Boyles shop and I was about 100 yds. away at the corner of the junction with Tullymore and Tullagh Park . This goon really annoyed me as he saw me aiming the rifle at him and his response was to drop his aim and give me the bird. All I could think was the cheeky bastard so I stepped out and gave him the Bird back he raised his weapon to firing position and I did the same I let him fire first and he missed by a whisker exploding a brick in the wall beside my head and then he stood there and let me fire but I didn't miss and as I disappeared up the back gardens I was thinking some of these cunts are as mad as me. The MRF/SAS were retaliating to our upsurge in attacks with their own, they did at least two drive by shootings and killed a couple of our volunteers from the Riverdale Area and we reckoned that this death squad was based in Casement Park. So we decided to sicken them and we put an IED on the waste ground that the Brits were using to cross into Riverdale and we got a jackpot we killed at least two of the patrol and wounded two or three more and one of the dead was The Officer in command of the fort Major Story who was at that time the highest ranking soldier to be killed in the troubles. It put a stop to their murderous incursions into Riverdale for a while at least. The Brits went ape shit about Story's croaking and we, realising that this was about to get uglier than normal went to our safe houses and kept our heads down. It wasn't long before a minor riot on Finaghy Road North turned out to be the vehicle for the Brits revenge when they shot and killed a young lad from De La Salle Secondary School who they claimed was throwing petrol bombs although this broke their own rules which forbade them from killing petrol bombers . It was a vicious tit for tat were we killed Security forces and they killed anyone they wanted.

In the meantime I was carpeted in work because my sick leave had been all used up and apparently I was heading for a very serious job review where I could be suspended for six months on two thirds pay and be given a strong letter of censure. The job was starting to get tough on staff who abused the system and their punishments had me shaking in my boots.

Most of my friends and comrades and I do mean most, didn't have the difficulty off living a double life, my friends weren't in the IRA and my comrades were in the IRA but didn't have a job. It makes life so much simpler when you only have to be one side of a coin. However as it transpired I was walking down one of the interminable corridors at work on my way to a compulsory tea break that was part of our job description when I saw a pair of painters and decorators busily painting a section of wall that had already been painted not more than a month ago. Now your normal punter would chuckle quietly to himself about the waste of tax payer's money in doing this, but when like me you have a hyper active sense of self-preservation you focus on other aspects of a situation like the word "busily". It was definitely forever since these old walls had seen anybody busily doing anything and I wouldn't say that alarm bells started going off in my head but a fucking Claxton went off in my ear. I started running in the opposite direction and I felt as though I was running through sand when in reality I was off like a hare and stopping for nothing. I came to a junction in the corridor and took the right hand fork which led to the basement. The two painters had thrown down all their painting gear produced a pistol each and were tearing after me, they weren't gaining but then again they weren't losing any ground either. I knew that one of the middle managers in the building was housed in a small office at the far side of the basement and beside the fact that he was a complete goon he was also a Captain in the UDR and that he always carried his service pistol with him in a supposedly concealed carry holster under his cardigan. The basement was the size of a football pitch and had tons of stuff that carried the dust of centuries. I knew my way through this maze fairly well as I spent a lot of time down here with a little red haired Protestant beauty who knew every position in the Kama Sutra. I tore around the final corner and there was Mr Jim as he liked to be called standing filling in some documents for a load of packages at his feet. Jim Help! Help! I yelled these IRA bastards are trying to kill me. Fuck the IRA he said and as fast as Billy the Fucking Kid a Browning appeared in his hand spitting death. Your two assassins never knew what hit them the bullets took them in the chest and head initially and when they had fallen to the ground good old Jim went around and shot them up the arse and any other demeaning place he could hit them. He was whooping and hollering obviously over joyed about the fact that he was now going to be some sort of hero among his friends. I knew it would come out sooner rather than later that the bold Jim had killed two of his comrades and his life would turn to shite.

CHAPTER 21:

I was more worried about the fact that this was now the fourth attempt on my life and no matter what else you say about them the SAS were dangerous enemies to have on your tail. It was now apparent to me that the next P Check or the next time I fell into the hands of the Brits I was going home in a box. So I carried a couple of guns with me at all times a Beretta 9mm and a Colt .32 Auto with a built in hammer so that I could keep it inside my jacket and it would never get stuck in my clothes when I needed to use it. Of course that was work finished and so was wandering around the area. I couldn't make up my mind whether it was better to travel by car or on foot and I always had one of the girls with me who scouted ahead of me when I was going from house to house. It also meant that going out socialising was definitely out of the question I couldn't even go to my ma's house as the Brits were raiding it regularly she couldn't even keep the carpet

tacked down as the Brits kept ripping it up. I was now the 1st Batt Operations Officer which was a pain in the ass because it meant going to meetings about this and that and that increased the probability that I would be taken or shot.

It was at this time that we got in new weapons that made the other weapons in our arsenal sort of redundant so we dumped them somewhere safe but accessible if they were ever needed but I knew that we would never see them or use them again. Away went all our old friends the WW1 gear , Martini Henrys ,Winchesters , Steyrs,.303s, Lewis guns, Mausers for fuck sake there where even muzzle loaders there. Also the WW2 gear went the same way.303s, Mausers, Garands, Thompsons ,M1Carbines,BARs, Stens,Grease Guns and a score of weird and wonderful guns that we had used to great effect. In came the Middle east gear starting with SKSs AK47s and including FNs, G3, MP5s, Styers and more American Gear M4s,M16 and M60s and other weapons more numerous to list here .We now had the best of weapons and could feel confident that our firepower could now match the Brits there was even a rumour that we would be getting SAMs. All this activity obviously attracted attention and it was apparent to us that the Brits had an inkling of what we were up to. As I was now known as what was called a red light meaning that the Brits wanted me preferably dead rather than alive I was a danger to anybody with me and it was decided that I would go to the Border counties were I was at least safe on the Free State side of the border when I wasn't operating. I soon realised that this wasn't my scene at all and I was getting messed around by people that didn't really want nor need my help. A typical example was the shooting off a well known orange man who was also a member of the UDR and lived on a farm about 2 miles from the Border. He was also suspect in the shooting dead of a local IRA member a few months previous. He continued to work his farm and be a part time member of the UDR although he was aware that he was a target and that the Provos had him in their sights and were determined to put him down for the dirt nap. Except the Security forces were aware of this and they were targeting us targeting him. His house was about 500 yds up a narrow lane and at the top of the lane there was a gate that he had to open on his way in and out and it was the ideal place to hit him not the only place but the ideal place. Of course he had taken serious precautions. It was obvious that we couldn't hit him at night because the lane was dark and there was no background light and beside this we were sure that he was under observation from an undercover SAS kill team who were set up to take us out should we be tempted to try. Also to do it in the morning was equally difficult as not only was there the suspected under cover squad to deal with but there was a helicopter up above surveying the whole area every morning which must have cost a fortune just to protect one man although his safety wasn't their only concern they were after us as well. Regardless of all this protection it was decided to have a go and kill him so we came up with the best plan possible. The neighbouring farm was about 600yds from his gate and was gone to wreck and ruin and the other farmers in the surrounding area used this land for grazing their cattle on and they often brought farm machinery there to salvage and cannibalise any of the redundant equipment they could for spare parts. The Brits were used to seeing the odd farmer in the vicinity of the old farm and took no notice so we sent one of the local lads in a tractor with a very large drill bit on the back of it to drill a seven foot deep hole in a clear area with a good line of sight about 400 yards from the gate. The hole was fitted out with all the mod cons a log was dropped in to use as a seat and to stand on to see over the top of the hole and a one foot deep box full of grassy sods was secured in the neck to cover the entrance. The idea of putting the hole in a clear area was twofold one to give me a clear shot and two was to hope that the Brits would bypass areas with no cover and search the areas with rough ground and natural camouflage. The idea was that I would get into the hole the previous night before the shooting and wait for the target until the next morning and top him when he got out of his car to open the gates .Then pull the cover over me and stay there until the coast was clear and someone came to get me but under no circumstances was I to climb out of the hole before the all clear was given, I reckoned about 24 hrs would be enough time to let things settle down. I had a choice of weapons and I wasn't used to being spoilt for choice , that was one of the many good things about the Border ASUs they were never short of good weapons and for this particular job I chose a Dragunov7.62x54mmR with a first class set of Optics and I carried a Beretta 9mm as my sidearm. I took a little pack with me consisting of a few sandwiches some chocolate bars and a 2 ltr bottle of water oh and I nearly forgot a small little flash lamp for emergencies and I was dressed in Irish Army DPMs. I had a couple of bowls of stew that filled me up and would stop my stomach rumbling for a while and then some of the lads drove me out as near to the ambush site as I could get and I had to hoof it from there to the hole on my own. I didn't waste any time getting there and dropping in when I discovered to my great annoyance that the hole was a quarter full of water and my boots and lower legs were soaking, there was nothing I could do but pull the lid partially over the top of me and wait for the dawn and my target. As I hadn't got the lid fully closed I could see the stars clearly in the blackness and I hummed a few tunes like Ten Guitars and Vincent to keep the Bogey Man away and keep the sense of rising panic under control. Sometime in the night about half past four I heard hushed voices coming from close to my position and I reckoned that the undercover SAS team were changing personnel and I sat absolutely still and hardly breathing until the stealthy noises had dissipated and I was on my own again. This was when I realised that the SAS team were in front of me and almost between myself and the target, there were a few scrubby little bushes off to my right about 200yds and that was really the only place they could get cover. This didn't make me a happy Bunny to realise that there was an SAS kill team within a short distance of me and they could be on me in seconds if any of them should be looking my way when I took the shot. The plan was going assways and the only choice I had was whether or not to take the shot. I nearly let my imagination get the better of me as I pictured the brits pulling open the lid of my hiding place and shooting down onto me or throwing a Hand grenade into the hole or worse still driving an armoured car forward and back over the entrance until I was buried alive like I had seen the Russians do to the Germans in WW2 Movies. I knew that I had to stop the panic and I did a little trick on myself that calmed me down, I visualised a Cigar box and into it one fear at a time I put my worries until they were all gone and then I put the box up onto a high shelf and left it there until the panic was long gone and I could open it up again in a controlled frame of mind. It was a trick taught to me by an old Indian called Jerks His Horses and I thought of all the ridiculous permutations I could think of LIke Chief Wanks the Worms and my all time favorite, Two dogs fucking. I could keep this up all night.

There was absolutely no chance of me falling asleep and I was so glad that I had worn a cap as countless little crawley things fell on top of me. The dawn came up at around 6/00am and I took a small pair of Binoculars out of one of my combat pockets and scanned the area between myself and where I imagined the undercover team would be but I couldn't see anything at all in the scrub so I started a grid search pattern and almost immediately spotted a slow methodical grinding motion and when I focused in on it I was certain that it was a jaw moving like someone chewing gum a bad mistake on their part, not very professional at all. I still couldn't see any other shapes or movement a credit to their camouflage but the area in which they were lying was too small to hold any more than two people. I was totally unsure about what to do should I cancel and bug out should I take the shot at the target or should I take out the target and the two SAS operatives as well. My primary concern was what would give me the best chance of survival and I couldn't make up my mind, The first option was not a runner. If I took that option I might never have come at all, it was a decision between the latter two and as I couldn't make up my mind I began to get angry. Suddenly my quandary was interrupted by the roar of the old farm land rover which meant that my target was on the way. I stayed focused on the gate and concentrated all my attention on the four hundred yard run up. Along he came on his daily ritual not realising it would be his last, when he got to the gate he climbed stiffly out of the cab and walked around to the front of the gate and opened it , then he stopped and turned to face the sun which was shining from directly behind me and put both his arms in the air and gave a mighty yawn and I squeezed the trigger and the rifle roared and bucked in my hands he, took the shot dead centre in his chest spun around and ran back up the lane but I knew he was fucked because I knew the shot was a winner the second the bullet left the muzzle, he started to slow down and through the scope I could see blood and intestines grouting out of his back. In a flash the SAS were up on their knees searching for the shooter panning their rifles back to back in two 180deg arcs trying desperately to pick up a target so I decided in that instant to go for broke and opened fire on the both of them I had nine rounds left in the rifle and I gave them the whole nine yards roughly half each which finished them. At the time I was tempted to make a run for it but there was nowhere to run too and I knew that to deviate from the plan unpleasant as it was, would be certain death. Anyway already I could hear the faint buzz of the helicopter coming in on my position so I took what might be my last look at the sun and with great reluctance pulled closed the cover on my little den and sat down to wait.

I never knew the meaning of the word wait until then. I expected to be in there about 24 hrs and I checked each hour that passed on my watch with the aid of my little torch and by the time 8 hrs had passed I thought it was a week. I tried to sleep but after a good snooze I found that I had only been asleep for about 20 minutes I then stopped looking at my watch as the slow march of time was only depressing me more and more. I then started a debate with myself about how I got myself into these positions and why did I always have to be the hero, I swore that if I got out of this I would be finished and retire. Finally I reasoned I had been in the hole about 20hrs and I was on the run in to being let out I checked my kit about 100 times to make sure I had cleaned up everything and even checked to make sure that my little nylon laundry bag which I had taped to the ejector of the Draganov had caught all my brass I even tried to think of something cool to say when they came to let me out but I was passed being smart I just wanted out of this fucking hole. No one came and the hours dragged by up to thirty hours in the hole and I was getting desperate I considered pushing off the lid and peeking out but somewhere inside myself I knew that there was a good reason why no one had come and to open up and to climb out would be suicidal. The time kept slowly crawling by and with a start I realised I had been in here for over 48 hrs. My feet were like blocks of ice and to make things worse if there was worse it had rained and the hole was starting to fill up with water. It had long ago covered the log on which I was sitting and was up to my waist. I decided to relax and die here and lost all track of time and found I really didn't care anymore. I must have gone semi unconscious when I heard a voice saying" holy fuck he's still alive" and hands reached in and pulled me free of my muck filled prison. Although I was physically Ok I was mentally a little unhinged and I just wanted to get away out to a big open space and run for miles. The lads explained to me what had happened, that immediately after the shootings the Brits had swamped the area with hundreds of troops and had set up their base less than 100 yds. From my position and searched all around it, they came close but never seemed in any danger of finding it, I could have cared less I was out and safe and free. I spent a lot of my time moving weapons around the country both north and south they may have caught the Claudia Gunship in March 73 but she had already done two trips to Ireland prior to that and the country was awash with weapons and it was getting safe places to hide them was the problem. The Brits were making great capital out of the amount of firearms being caught after operations but the fact was The IRA were telling ASUs to throw away their weapons after use as they had so many spare weapons that large amounts of them were now surplus to requirements and lots of volunteers took weapons to keep as personals just in case whatever ever happened.

The lads in the ASU called down to see me in County Monaghan and I realised that I really didn't like it on the Border so without a bye your leave I jumped a lift back to Andytown and decided to take my chances at home. The lads were more content with me back in the saddle again and I started my new regime called Staying Alive. I reasoned that I was less likely to get stiffed when I was operational as at least then I was armed and prepared.

The period of time most dangerous for me and any other Volunteer on the run was travelling from place to place for example between call houses or safe houses to attend meetings or to make arrangements for upcoming jobs and if like me you were a Red Card you might as well go as heavily armed as you could because if you were caught you would probably be executed anyway.

I came back to Andytown just at the right time and slipped straight back into my previous roll. I had been called to a meeting in a house on the Glen Road where we were told that something big was in the pipeline and that I would be briefed separately about it but that in the meantime it was all hands to the pumps for the week leading up to Friday we were told to go out and score as many hits as we were able and there were no restrictions and we had Carte Blanch to hit any targets we could. This was unprecedented for us it was over six months since we had this sort of freedom so I got the two Andytown ASUs together and we made up four teams off three. The best way to get multiple fast results was shoot and scoot, in fact it was the only way I mean how hard can it be if you are three to a car well, armed and you have a target rich environment which means every one coming under your gun from Protestant civilians, Protestant paramilitaries to all Security Force members. If you can't score in this scenario you shouldn't be in the republican movement. I told the four teams that the least I would accept was one body each and I didn't want to hear any fuckin excuses, this sort of pressure certainly sorts out the wheat from the chaff.

Our first score was the next day a Sunday, Team 1 got a Brit in Joy St in the Markets and a Loyalist Paramilitary on the Lisburn Road on the way back. Also on Sunday Team 2 shot and killed a Brit in Little Distillery St off the Grosvenor Road a solid piece of work considering the shot that took him out was a tad over 300yds. On Tuesday Team 3 scored two UDA men manning a barricade off the top of the Ormeau Road and stiffed both of them. On Thursday my team put the icing on the cake when we shot dead a Brit in Divis Drive and he turned out to be the one hundredth British Soldier to be shot dead since the start of the troubles. I gave the lads a great well done and many thanks from

1st Batt staff but what they appreciated more was the hooley we threw the following night when they realised what the show was for.

CHAPTER 22:

As they say change is the mother of invention and after the ceasefire the Brits came out with new tactics, they had been busy during the Ceasefire where as we had spent our time drinking and whoring and the rest of the time we had squandered. The Brits did something that really shocked us and the bastards played on our last nerve. When they finished their patrolling for the day only about half of them went back to the fort the other half disappeared and they stopped patrolling at nights. They just disappeared into unoccupied houses into communal garages, back gardens, alleyways and waste ground. In effect they left the nights to us to do with as we wanted and seeing as we were used to sleeping at night and we had no night vison equipment the nights were pretty useless to us. As well as that when we came out in the morning to begin our gunman stuff there were little pockets of Brits all over the place just waiting with itchy trigger fingers for us to make a mistake.

It was obvious that they couldn't keep it up they hadn't the manpower to cope and even though they were saving a bit by not putting out night patrols the number crunching definitely had to show a deficit of available hours. On top of this it was fucking cold at night in Andytown and the poor Brits suffered colds and sneezes and cried off sick in increasing numbers. It was at a time like this that the Fianna came into its own we had at least 100 of the wee buggers and they searched the estate from top to bottom for covert Brit posts. They kicked footballs into back gardens and then followed up with a through search to find it again, they broke into empty houses and ransacked them they turned the Brits out of their hiding places like rats. I'd say whoever thought of this strategy got booted up and down the Barracks and were laughed all the way back to Sandhurst or whatever upper crust goon factory they were trained in.

Not long after this we ambushed an open top Jeep on the Stewartstown road and missed by a mile although we got our first sighting off the latest regiment to enter the war in Andytown" a regiment the Devil calls his own, known as the Black Watch and commissioned by the throne". In all honesty they were nothing special in combat terms in fact I would consider them to be below average in both training and height and they certainly were the Regiment of Poisoned Dwarfs we came to know and hate. They were Huns to the core and Glasgow Rangers supporters to boot and they hated Fenians and Celtic supporters with equal ferocity. They revelled in doing spiteful and humiliating things like slapping you repeatedly across the face when you were getting P Checked which we were at least 2/3 times a day, taking lads lunches off them on their way to work and spitting or snotting in them and they suffered with little man syndrome. They loved to hold big guys at gunpoint and offer them a fair dig though there was nothing fair in it as soon as you hit back six or seven of the evil dwarfs would set about you and kick your keek in. It gave us an extra special incentive in shooting them up and we really got great satisfaction in hitting some of the worst ones, like a wee fucker we nicknamed Tich who specialised in humiliating every woman he encountered. I shot him through the mouth on Slieveban Hill which put a final stop to his antics and gave the Brits a lesson in not sticking your head above the parapet.

In general the further south in England the Regiments came from the more laid back they were the Guards(Irish) in particular are a fairly decent bunch as Brits go, London and the surrounding areas are full of live and let live squaddies who like the soldier who saw the gun underneath the suit jacket and said nothing. The Welsh Fusiliers aren't too bad it was one off their officers who arranged a meeting with the 1st Batt Staff in Andersonstown and told us plainly that their men would not fire unless fired upon and there would be the very minimum P checking and house to house raiding. It was the quietist four month tour of duty in the whole of the troubles in N Ireland. However the day after they moved out the Gordon Highlanders moved in and there was a proverbial shit storm partly because it was the Gordons whom we hated and also because we had spent the last four months like caged lions too proud to be the ones to break our word.

It was late September and the nights were starting to draw in, I wasn't keen on this time of the year I'm sure John Keats was bang on when he said that Autumn was "a season of mists and mellow fruitfulness" and how he thought it was fab and all this Bolloxology, but I didn't agree with him, I remember writing a review in Sixth class in De La Salle on this very same bucko and the general gist of my review was that John Keats was an effete snob and a Homo to boot. Unfortunately my Form Brother, Brother Wally thought while my review was original and interesting, if I handed in shit like this again I'd be out of A level English and picking up papers in the yard with the Retard class 5Z or something like that. I think Brother Wally was a Homo or a kiddy fiddler but you couldn't say things like that at that time or your Da would have kicked you up and down the school yard before what was left of you was given to the Brothers for training in extra Religious Education every night after school so that they could break your spirit and you could give them the odd Blow Job like a good lad. The only blow job they ever got from me was when I and a few of my merry band sneaked into the school one night on the 7of August 1972 with 2 RPG,s and a 50lb bomb and attacked the School Gymnasium which the Brits were using as a billet, I think we killed and wounded about 11 or 12 Green Jackets or Green Howards that night. Anyway I was about to explain before I got side tracked by La Salle School the reasons we didn't like fighting in the winter, because it was dark and the

Brits had too big an advantage in the dark, they had night vision and could see us clearly were as we could see sod all. So we tried to compress our operations into the few daylight hours after people finished work but this was to constraining and telegraphed the timing of our jobs to the brits and our old friend Zero was very quick to cop onto this but we copped as soon as he copped because we had Curleys dad still monitoring the Brits radio traffic for us, he did a hell of a job even though he was terminally ill with cancer and he was the cause of a number of Brits biting the dust and saved a number of our operatives including myself being warned off about the position of Brit foot patrols and ambush sites. The girls bought us all black outfits Jeans, Polo neck Jumpers and Bomber Jackets an appropriate name for them I think and in my humble opinion we looked the Bee's Knee's real hard men, hard on the nappies would be more like it. We used the black like Camo Gear and we thought that we looked like IRA ninjas sure we even argued about who looked most like Bruce Lee. On one occasion after opening up on a brit foot patrol I ran up an entry and into a back garden and as I tore across the garden I ran into a washing line and nearly fuckin garrotted myself. On another occasion I jumped over back garden wall and landed on top of a greenhouse which left me an ass full of glass and needing stitches. The worst however was when I ran across a couple of back gardens and into the yard of a guy who bred Rottweilers and I had to shoot two of them to get away they nearly ate me alive. I decided that this strategy was going nowhere and we needed to try something new. Oh just as an aside my buddy Clinger had come back from the dead and I was honestly glad to see him, he went back to being my driver and wingman and Curley reverted to his position as QM and spare shooter. Clinger was chock full of new ideas that he had come up with while lying in Hospital down south while he made a speedy recovery. Most of his ideas were frankly insane, suicidal or both. One that I dismissed initially was for six of us with handguns to spread out and walk casually along a busy main road falling in behind a Brit Foot Patrol and when the signal was given like a whistle blast to shoot the soldier in front of you in the head. Everybody including me roared with laughter and Clinger took the needle. We asked him was he sure it was the stomach he was shot in and was he sure it wasn't the head. He kept on pushing the idea every chance he got he got and even went above my head to Battalion for which I gave him a root up the hole. Eventually I began to see some merit in it. Not only could we kill six Brits but that we could take out a whole patrol which from a propaganda standpoint would be a huge coupe. It would be like the disappearance of the 9th legion by them bloody Picts and Scots the evil buggers except we did'nt have a Golden Eagle to go missing the closest we could come would be our Polly whom we kept locked in a cage she was one of those Belfast killer budgies who used go for your face and get tangled in your hair and shite all over you. So we practiced the situation as often as we could but we could never to manage to guarantee any more than 3 Brits because of the cover system they used which would leave the other 3 Brits too much time to think and get their shit together fast enough to return fire. The best we were getting was 3 for 3 and they weren't good odds at all.

While we were searching for other ways to tackle the Brits in the dark we were instructed to attend a very urgent meeting this meant all of us with no exceptions, it was to be held in a safe house in Gransha Park and we were informed that 2 other ASU's were also to attend that meant that there would be circa 20 volunteers in attendance which was insane, not only would we lose 20 men if the house got raided. Not only that but our carefully controlled security would be blown asunder and everybody would know the identity of all the ASU members in the area. I complained about the stupidity of this meeting but was told that it was a direct order from GHQ staff. On the day of the meeting we went armed to the teeth we made sure that if things went arseways and the Brits raided the house we could fight our way out there was no fuckin way we would get captured without a fight. On the day of the meeting rumours were rife, civil war, ceasefires, and surrender were only a few of the reasons muted for the meeting I was a little nervous myself about what could be so important you would risk 20 volunteers to pass on information.

At the appointed time in came an old time Republican whom I recognised as Tom MC Call a stalwart of the Easter Rising and the war of Independence. He was in a very sombre mood and he pulled up a chair facing us looked us full in the face and in his most authoritarian tones he said I'm here on the orders of the GHQ staff off the Republican Movement to talk to you about sex.There was a stunned silence and then everyone roared with laughter accompanied by such comments as more sex for volunteers, free love, ride her cowboy and yahoo wee doggies, someone had obviously been watching to many westerns. The old man sat in stoney silence and waited for the uproar to die down. He continued on to explain to us that this was no laughing matter because too many of our female volunteers were getting pregnant and this was bringing the Republican Movement into disrepute. GHQ Staff had decided that anyone breaking the rules should be stood down pending a court-martial and could be dismissed from the movement. There was a shocked silence and then I said who are you kidding we haven't got enough volunteers to fight the Brits as it is without losing people over this non sense. Then questions came hot and heavy excuse the pun and somebody shouted up what about skins can we use them, what about putting all the birds on the pill, what if you just give it to her up the arse, is a blow job out of the question etc etc ect. To say old Tom was shocked and stunned would be an understatement he fled the room never to be seen again. We heard that he went to GHQ Staff and ratted us out but as always happens they were caught up in something else and worries about sex had gone out the window. When the girls heard about this they went out of their way to push their Boobs and asses at us to try to cause us embarrassment which it didn't. As it happened Clinger fucked a Cumman Na Mban girl the following week and she complained about it and said he got her drunk he said you couldn't have gotten her drunk with a gallon off Bacardi and she cost him a fortune for the ride. I reckoned that you would want to have a strong stomach to tackle this one as she was a Beast of The Pampas.Clinger never had any luck with women he was painfully shy and a Ginger Minger to boot and his chat up lines left a lot to be desired one of his problems was that he was too desperate for a ride and he was forever picking one bird or another and following her around like a wee puppy he was giving a gun lecture in a house one day and was trying to impresss one of the girls there when he cocked an MP3A1grease gun which he then handed to her and told her to put the safety on but the safety was tight and she was nervous and she dropped the gun on the floor and it went off spinning around in a circle on the floor and it never stopped until it had fired the last round, some of us had jumped onto chairs and threw ourselves onto the table and two of the volunteers were hopping around the floor like Fred Astaire and Ginger Rogers on a mad one.

CHAPTER 23:

A new batch of RPG 7's had arrived we called all the RPG's 7 but what we actually had been using was the RPG2. The 7's were the up dated version of the 2's but we were having problems with them and getting misfires. Three of us were sent to a training camp to update ourselves on the new weapon so I picked my two buddies Clinger and Curley and we hired a Ford Transit van from Mc Causlands car hire on a false licence and a couple of hours later we were on our way to the wilds of Co Clare. Other than being stopped at the British Army checkpoint and being waved through we had an uneventful trip down. We pulled into a little village on the coast of Clare and went into the local Takeaway for a bite to eat. I was just looking at the menu over the counter when I saw two girls I knew from Belfast and after a quick what are you doing here they told me they were down on an Engineering course for two days and they were staying in the same place as us. The cottage we were staying in was a summer rental for tourists who wanted to get peace and tranquillity and there was nowhere as peaceful and tranquil as here. The people who owned the house supplied us with food and drinks but sadly no alcohol was allowed, they also loaned me a Colt .45 in case the Garda or Irish army came around and we had to fend for ourselves. We spent two intense days there and learned what we needed. As it turned out the differences between the RPG 2 and the PRG 7 were minimal and in all seriousness we didn't have had to come all this way to be show what we could have picked up in Belfast in five minutes. The camp only lasted one day so we said Slan ` to the girls and headed home. The drive home was as relaxed as it was coming down and we only got stopped twice once by the Garda and once by the Brits and both times they only checked Clingers licence and waved us through, it was a lot to do with impressions both on the way down and up we were wearing football tops and the car was full of balls and hurls and other such paraphernalia, sports connected and all the Brit saw looking into the car was three football players on their way to a game. Times get tough and the few get fewer I think it was oul Winston who said "Never in the field of human conflict was so much been owed by so many to so few" even though the words were spoken by an English man the sentiment felt relevant to us. There was a reception committee waiting for us when we got back and somebody in Brigade had complained about our little trip to Co Clare and that our business was out fighting a war and not swanning around on little junkets. So I told them not to worry that we would fight the war and leave the Junkets to them obviously they had lots of experience in enjoying themselves and time wasting.

I decided it was time to get back to normal operations and with Clinger back we could plan the type of jobs we were good at so we decided to get totally traditional and pull off a shooting at the junction of Kenard Ave and Tullymore Gdns we planned it for a Friday morning , myself and Clinger would do the shooting and Curley would supply the car which he would park on the front of Shaws Road about two thirds of the way from the turnoff at Rosnareen Flats and facing downhill. This was a carbon copy of an ambush we had done previously and we all took up our positions with practiced ease. One well trusted and tried Fianna boy watched the top of Rossnareen flats and he was to ensure we wern't spotted by a patrol coming down the main road behind us and he had his trusty whistle for giving the alarm. Curley covered the bottom of Tullymore hill where it intersected Edenmore Drive and Greenan and the same applied to him he was to whistle if the Brits came up the hill which would effectively trap us on both sides and leave us boxed in with the car ok but nowhere to drive it as the junction at the bottom of the Shaws and Andytown roads would be blocked. This was to be our runback, down the Shaws right up Stewartstown Rd and left into Trench House Teachers Training College and round at the back was a big shed were the students stored lots of canoes into which we could throw the weapons and cover them with swim jackets and paddles which would keep them hidden unless the Brits found some reason to search them. All we had to do after getting rid of the weapons was to drive back down the driveway and turn left up Stewartstown Rd and into Lenadoon to a safe house. But there is all ways the last one thing left, Murphys Law, what can go wrong will go wrong. We took up our positions Clinger was about 50yds up from me and taking cover behind a low concrete wall about 5 ft in height from where he would see the Brits as they came down the street I was lying on the side path off a house looking directly up the street and I would see them first and let them get to about 20yds from Clinger which was 70yds from me and I would fire first with the Scoped Jungle .303and take out the first man on the patrol and then Clinger was to open fire with the Armalite hopefully hitting at least one of them but definitely keeping their heads down until I could get out of the very exposed position that I had adopted. I had warned Clinger twice that he wasn't to fire until I had fired first because I would only get off one shot with the .303 before I would have to run up the side path of the house through the back yard and garden climb the back wall into the next garden and cut across its backyard and run up its back side wall into the front garden and across the little Green at the front of the house and get into the car parked on the front of the road. Clinger would have to do exactly the same thing as me except after he let go his first shot he had to keep firing as he ran so the noise of the shooting would keep the Brits pinned down and help to cover my runback as well as his own altough just in case of an emergency I had a Colt.45 pistol in my pocket to give me emergency firepower if I needed it. I hoped to Jesus I didn't .

Myself and Clinger picked up the car and drove around the block to make sure that everybody was present and correct. Curley was in position and so was the Fianna scout who gave us a wee salute as we drove past him I'd explain to him later that we didn't salute in the IRA. Finally we got around to the parking space for the car right on the front of the road and some Gobshite had parked in it. There was a little layby just in the spot we wanted which would have kept the car looking natural parked on the main road but now we had to park the car sitting nearly blocking the left hand lane and looking suspicious as hell. Once the car was parked as best we could manage we got out and locked it and left the key on top the front tyre in the wheel arch this was in case we dropped or lost the key or one of us having the key was unable to make it back. Yea we hoped to Jesus that didn't happen either. The weapons were on the back seat of the car and we shared them out shoved them up our jackets and headed down to our chosen positions we had only climbed over the first gate when we ran into a woman hanging out washing who nearly fainted when she saw us, I grabbed her by the arm and told her that we were the Irish Republican Army and she was to get inside until the shooting g was over and if I found out she had raised the alarm in any way I would personally kill her. She swore that she wouldn't say a word and disappeared into the house like she was never there. Then Clinger started moaning " I have a bad feeling about this job maybe we should call it off and try something else" I told him to fuck up and dry his eyes that we were going to do this job no matter what. This is where in all modesty you need someone like me on a job because I just bulldoze over any problems and I always get the job done, improvise and adapt I'm like the hound of the Baskervilles once released somebody gets killed, and I never come back with an excuse about why we had to call a job off. So after telling Clinger in no uncertain terms that the job was going ahead he stowed his nerves and got on with the operation. We made our way to our respective firing positions to get settled in and ready. I glanced up to see a fucking audience peeking out their back bedroom windows were obviously we had been spotted getting into position. There were people looking frightened, some excited and there were some giving us silent thumbs up, I hoped Clinger wouldn't notice them or this would be another excuse and gripe. I got to the side path I was using as my firing position and lay down and took a look through my sights and picked out exactly were on the side fence that the first Brit would walk along that I was going to fire. That done I checked my rifle to make sure there was a round up the spout and made sure that the safety catch was off. That was a big difference between us and the Brits, no matter when I had a gun in my possession I had the weapon cocked and the safety off. It meant that in a life or death situation which it always was we always fired fastest and first and if we let rip in error it was too bad for anyone in the firing line we were fighting a war and bad things happened. The most you would have gotten for shooting some poor sod in error was a slap on the wrist. The sun had come up and it was getting uncomfortably warm so I squeezed in underneath the hedge which ran along the side of the house for shade, I was lying there running through the attack in my head and sweating like a whore when I heard the crackle of a Brit radio close to me, fuck I realised that I had been sleeping and jumped to my feet while sighting up the rifle and taking up the whole optic was a Brit my target and not 15yds from me .He saw me at the same time as I saw him and the shock on his face was instant and terrible and as I had just been explaining I was locked and loaded and fired immediately I saw the bullet hit him in the chest not so much any movement on his part or a hole appearing anywhere he just dropped to the ground like a rag doll and never moved again in this life. Some of the other members of the Patrol caught a glimpse of me moving and opened fire and there was a thunder of firing that seemed never to stop and brick chippings and bullets flew through the air I ran up the back gardens and the Brits ran after me firing until they had emptied their mags. I was cursing

Clinger because it was for this reason he had an Armalite with a 30 round mag in it he was supposed to be my cover and I couldn't hear the crack of the Armalite anywhere near me, I took the Colt out of my pocket and returned fire on the Brits who weren't to keen on charging ahead now that I was shooting back. I legged it out to the car and never even looked to see where Clinger was I just assumed that he was in the car waiting on me but he wasn't I jumped out again and felt for the key and it was still there, I knew that this meant that Clinger was still out there in the middle of at least two patrols of soldiers. I thought about what to do for what seemed an eternity while the Brits raked on, what they were firing at fuck knows it wasn't me and it was too far down to be Clinger. So I decided to be a hero or an ejit or something in between so I threw the rifle into the back seat of the car and holding the pistol ran down through the back gardens to find Clinger however the brits saw me again and a whole new shit load of firing resumed only I was the target this time. For those of you who have fought house to house Brits included the noise is something else it's not like firing in the countryside were flat wide open spaces disperse the sound it's like a gun battle inside a steel drum and you get temporary deafness. As dire as the situation was it was like a Monty Python Sketch, I was running around chasing Brits and looking for Clinger and there were Brits chasing me and shooting at each other. I was just getting to the point where I would have to give up the attempt to save Clinger when I heard his voice just behind a wall in front of me and I vaulted over it and there God bless him was Clinger. Unfortunately standing in the firing position with his rifle pointed right at Clingers chest was a Baby Brit all dressed up and kitted out to look like a soldier in all honesty I would have kicked his arse and sent him on his way but the poor fucker remembered just enough of his training to get himself killed, in his panic he swung toward me and started to fiddle with the cocking action of his gun while at the same time shouting for help in a voice choked with fear and he left me with no alternative but to put three in his chest. I grabbed Clinger by the collar and we ran through a hail of gunfire back to the car I shouted at him to fire the Armalite at anything just to keep the Brits heads down and give us a chance to make it to the car. As we ran across the little green space to the car I could hear the gunfire getting more and more intense, we were gone so they were obviously shooting at each other. The two of us threw our weapons into the car and then climbed in after them we had lost a lot of time and despite them shooting at each other there had got to be a dozen or more patrols converging on the area and I definitely did not want to be here when they arrived. So with Clinger at the wheel and driving calmly we took off down the Shaws Road the turn at the bottom of the road was only around a couple of hundred yards away and the entrance to Trench House was only a hundred yards beyond that again we hadn't enough time to change our plan so we stuck to it and hoped for the best. As we drove up the driveway there wasn't a soul in the place there were no parked cars and no people wandering about that we could blend in with we stuck out like sore thumbs and I could hear that the shooting had stopped. There was little time left for the niceties of throwing paddles and flotation jackets down the canoes to hide the guns we just fucked them in and got out of there. As we drove out from behind the storage sheds two lines of Brits were running up the driveway toward us I could hear Clinger saying shit very quietly. All I could think off was how royally screwed we were I told Clinger to slow down and stop and as the car rolled to a stop we wound down our windows a number of the Brits ran past the car and up into Trench House but two of them stopped one on either side at each window and started hammering questions at us " where have you been , what were you doing there, were are you going ,did you hear shooting ,did you see anybody they never gave us time to answer the questions , I was busily explaining to the Brit on my side of the car that we were Trainee teachers and Clinger had tears in his eyes moaning that we were caught in the middle of a gun fight and were going to get shot ,the Brits looked at each other and then at us snivelling in the front of the car and waved us on and down onto the Stewartstown Road were we turned left to safety anyway it was the only turn we could make as the Brits had the right turn blocked. Clinger I said are they real tears, he replied that Spencer Tracy had nothing on him. I think the term Friendly Fire really applied to the Brits that day as they were shot mostly by their own or else with the amount of shots fired by the Brits into the air the seagull population of Andytown took a fair hammering. Once we were on the way up the Stewartstown Road toward Lenadoon we felt safe and we began to laugh at our narrow escape and we thought it was too hilarious for words, our nerves were shot to bits and we giggled like a pair of schoolgirls the whole way up the road. The safe house we had picked was across the road from a house with a telephone in it and less than a half hour after we had arrived a wee girl came across the road to us to tell us that Curleys dad was on the phone . After the shooting he had apparently ran up Tullymore Hill when he heard the extent of the Gun battle that was taking place and he had opened fire with a pistol he was carrying on a patrol of Brits that he had seen coming out of the Garages just before the corner of Kenard Ave thinking he was drawing some of the fire off us and onto himself. One off Curleys problems was that he had more balls than brains and was inclined to rush in where angels fear to tread. Now we had a major problem on our hands as he had been seen by the Brits going into a house for cover and was now surrounded. I couldn't think of any way to help him but at the same time he had gotten himself into this position trying however much misguidedly to help us. His Da had been monitoring events on the short wave radio and knew his son was trapped and worse the Brits weren't likely to take any prisoners after the hiding we had just given them. The OC from F Company Lenadoon and his brother came to our safe house to offer their services in any way they could short of digging a friggin tunnel under the house. His Da was frantic and was

145

constantly ringing the phone across the road with updates picked up from the Brits radio chatter.

The latest development was that a goon squad of plain clothes Brits had arrived at the house and I realised that they were going to storm it soon and Curleys days were numbered I hoped that he would try to surrender but I knew him too well and I knew he would shoot it out until the end. My mind was racing and I determined not to let Curley die without a fight on our part apparently his Da had sent me a message realising how hopeless the situation was and told me that he understood if I was unable to help. In anyway and always I came up with a Cunning Plan and got in touch quickly with the Lenadoon OC and told him what we needed and good as his word he came up Trumps in record time. The first the brits realised that something was up was when they heard the roar of a big fuckin diesel engine and a Tipper truck with Clinger driving and me in the back with a GPMG and two of the Lenadoon lads ripping it up with FN's came barrelling down the hill firing in all directions, crashed through the front garden pulled up outside the house and Curley threw himself into the back of the lorry. The Brits were running for cover as Clinger gunned the engine and we took off down the hill and were in the middle of Lower Andytown before the Brits could react. "I told you I had a bad feeling about this operation", Clinger said to which my reply was " would you ever shut the fuck up, Tiny Tears".

The Brits having been deprived of their prey when they could all but taste it came out in force and battered Adults, Teenagers and kids alike and vented their spleen on the population of Andytown but we stayed away and let them have a consolation prize.

 The Brits had taken the hump big time or else somebody higher up had got a size 9 up the hole for the miserable results that were being turned in and I'd say your average squaddie was getting it in the neck just because shit flows downhill. In the end the current regiment's tour was up and they stayed in their forts for the last few days before they beat an ignominious retreat back to Blighty. The next lot came in two regiments at the same time and this made life extremely difficult for us there were Patrols everywhere and we were nearly confined in our safe houses,

CHAPTER 24:

It was a major logistical operation just to change Billets. There were about ten of us on the run in the Andytown area who were actually on active service and at least another dozen who declared themselves to be on the run for fear they might get lifted by the Japs and spill the beans whilst being interrogated. There were even two or three who were on the run because they knew someone who knew someone who had hijacked a bus or some shite such as this. This sounds ridiculous until these asswipes start using the Army girls to scout for them around to the shops and back and up and down to their Ma's house for dinner. The girls were complaining to us and we in turn resolved the problem by telling everyone who didn't think they could stand up to interrogation by the Japs, should report to us immediately and we would execute them in advance to avoid any chance they might have to turn informer in the future. It solved the problem in double quick time I can tell you. There was even one thick that turned up to be shot and we sent him as far away as possible to Co Kerry in fact were in later years he married a farmer's daughter' had a dozen kids and lived happily ever after I've wondered since then who was the Thick him or us.

In all seriousness we would not have been able to fight the war without the Army Women and the Cumann na mBan you have only to take a look at the Roll of Honour to see how many died for Ireland and suffered torture, imprisonment and injustice at the hands of the British. I am privledeged to have known the few that I did.With the Brits having nearly doubled their normal manpower on the streets of Andytown at any one time, they were suffocating us and making even relatively simple jobs like shoot and scoot a major chore. It was clear that we needed some help from the other Battalions to put the Brits under pressure in their own areas and try and draw them away from us, as another consequence of this pressure was that Andytown being our largest dump for weapons, we were fast running out of munitions. A tour of duty for the Brits was four months and there was no way that the pressure could be kept at this intensity for the full duration off a tour. The other Battalions got stuck in and Ballymurphy came up trumps as usual along with the Lower Falls the Markets and the Strand. Also we decided to take an in depth look at what we were doing and to try and up our game. We reasoned that if it was too difficult to put on lots of small operations then we would put on one big job that would have them crying in their soup. Our first order of business was to contact our IO squad and make them earn their pay for a change and earn it they did. They came up with two targets that we could hit simultaneously that weren't in Andytown that would cause maximum embarrassment and would scare the living fuck out of the high and mighty and force the Brits to deploy hundreds of troops from the like of Andytown to patrol the streets of the more affluent areas of Belfast before they became the more effluent. They gave us the addresses, photographs, times in and out and details of security and bodyguards. All we were left with was to plan the attacks and get reliable volunteers to carry them out and I just happened to have the very men for the jobs. Meanwhile time was of the essence as the two Brit regiments now policing in Andytown were the Green Jackets and the Devon and Dorset's. The latter we at first didn't take seriously as they nearly all spoke like characters from the Pirates of Penzance with arrghs, bugger me and me hearty's and the black spot for the blind Pew maybe a tad exaggerated but you can imagine waiting at a P check for the Brit on the radio to say Yaarp. Despite their cute accent they were no fools and in conjunction with the Green Cowards were scooping up a large number of people who were going into Castlereagh and from there to Long Kesh. It doesn't matter that the majority of the lads scooped were new volunteers and fairly inexperienced what matters was they were our replacements and their loss was proving catastrophic for the continuity of the war effort. The Brits used to identify players and kill or capture them and fast track these known individuals to the cemetery or Internment. Now they were just Interning lads by the dozens and most of them were not involved in the struggle and were in for association only. Short term we were losing but in terms of the long game we were really winning, as the song goes "I went in a boy and came out a man " plus a very highly trained man who was now committed to the cause and had received the best Guerrilla warfare training from the best in the business. An always and anyways things weren't getting better out there and it was starting to look black round the coal quays so we decided to push this operation along as fast as possible and hope for the best outcome possible. We were an operative short, we needed four operatives and the only ones I could trust implicitly were Myself, Clinger and Curley however there was a Fianna boy who had proved his worth on a number of occasions, well when I say Fianna boy, he was a rather hairy assed fianna boy of about twenty two or so and he had been patiently waiting a place in the army, so we decided to give him a chance on one of the most dangerous jobs we had done in a long time. Like all of us his real name is of no importance to those of us in the movement and even then our real names were not that important either.

As operations go they are only as important as you make them and this one required two hijacked cars and the drivers held hostage for a maximum off two hours and then threatened with dire consequences if they went to the cops in less than an hour after their release. Each car would have a team of two a shooter and a driver the driver would pull the car up as close to the target house as possible and the shooter dressed up in a Postman's Uniform would casually walk down the Driveway with his mail sack on his shoulder and ask for the target by specifying that he had a registered letter which must be singed for by the

Addressee only. The other shooting was to be a carbon copy of the first which was why the assassinations would have to be timed almost perfectly even though they were miles apart less an alarm call go out by radio to the bodyguards that each of the High Court Judges had with them at all times. Curley did the shooting and El Tonto did the driving and as luck would have it the Judge himself opened the door and Curley whacked him stone dead before he even recognised what was taking place.

Clinger and myself had a much more difficult time everything went according to plan until the door was opened by a teenage girl who didn't seem to understand the rules governing postal etiquette and was insisting that I give her the letter. Finally she gave in and called for the Bodyguard to take the letter from me , he came out of the kitchen munching on a piece of toast and with hardly a glance at me he knew he was a dead man he tried to shout a warning and go for his gun at the same time and made a balls off both actions so I gave him two slugs in the chest as I ran past him and the screaming girl and into the kitchen, Your Honour was trying to pull a pistol from a kitchen drawer when I ran in and blew his head all over the table I'd imagine there were bloody beans for breakfast. As I ran back up the hall the young girl was still screaming and the RUC bodyguard was making a chesty puffing noise so I plugged him again to make sure he was croaked and then ran to Clinger who was in the getaway car and had the engine idling as he waited on me. As we took off a marked Police car fell in behind us and put the screamers on, he must have been close by and heard the shots and now we had a serious problem. It wouldn't take long for a chopper to get on top off us and start zeroing in the ground intercept units to box us in. Clinger was doing a 100mph on the straights and 60mph to 70mph on the bends but the Black Bastards we still hanging in and I doubted we were going to have the speed in the old Volvo Estate to out run them. It's at times like this that a professional driver is invaluable and Clinger was a professional. He shouted to me to get ready to shoot at their car and then he did something I was convinced was insane, he slammed on the brakes after we had just turned a corner and rammed the gear stick into reverse, their car ploughed into the back of ours and the Goon in the passenger seat came out through the window, I opened fire on them and Clinger rammed the car into drive and we took off leaving the pursuit car a total shambles on the road. The six o clock news that evening gave out the usual sympathetic bullshit but it also said the thing we most wanted to hear, in response to calls from Loyalist Politicians security was going to be beefed up in a number of Loyalist areas and guess who was going to do the beefing none other than our old buddies the Green Cowards which left us, with the Devon and Dorset's or the custard soldiers as we called them.

The effect was instantaneous and Andytown was open for business again, except the British establishment had gone apeshit and were lifting hundreds of lads for interrogation in a desperate attempt to find the culprits, which they never did. I'd say Willie Whitelaw saw the writing on the wall and surmised that his job was now forfeit and it would only be a matter of time until some other unfortunate received the Poison Chalice. I was told more than once that I was a great soldier but a political moron so I wouldn't quote my political ramblings as accurate but more guessed.

Too often now I was having close calls, but I didn't want to go to the Border again as I had enough the last time. However I had a premonition that my time was running out for instance two of us were leaving a house after a meeting and I thought that the other volunteer had checked outside and he thought I had a simple mistake. He stepped outside the front door and saw the Brits across the road and he instantly turned back into the house I knew it was a was an error and so did he but we were left with only one option but to run for the back door out of the house and hope there were no Brits in the back gardens but there were, he wasn't armed but I was and I opened fire right away, the Brits dived for cover and I went one way and he went another fortunately the direction I took was clear and I went up the back gardens like an Olympic hurdler and never looked back he unfortunately ran straight into a patrol and was captured and apparently the hiding they gave him was inhuman, they broke his jaw, both of his legs broke his nose and probably would have killed him only for the fact that loads of people came out of their houses and gave out to the Brits about their brutality oblivious of the fact that I had shot to kill didn't matter sometimes the Brits just couldn't win. As my Ma often said if you live by the sword you will die by the sword and we weren't like the media crying every time one of us got killed we were out to kill them as well and the lads who did the killing gave no quarter and expected none. There was hardly a day went past when we didn't encounter the Brits weather it was a couple of jeeps driving past while you were walking from one place to another or travelling in a car and running into a road block always armed of course

and just praying that yours wouldn't be the 3rd, 4th or 5th car they had as their searching pattern for that day. Or the choppers that were constantly hovering up there with the supposed magic camera systems that could see the fillings in your teeth. All this doesn't sound too stressful until you factor in that this is day after day, week after week, month after month and year after year. It affects people in different ways, some become paranoid and afraid and hardly leave their safe houses and others get angry and reckless and actively seek out insane confrontations like Berserkers of Viking Mythology.

To get a balance despite all the madness around you is a hard thing to achieve and to be fair and objective when even young as you are, you have the power to make decisions of life and death from shooting suspected informers to allowing jobs to go ahead that you shouldn't do, to just picking ordinary civilians out of a crowd and gunning them down. Sometimes you wonder will your end come as quickly as the end you have given others, one second your full of life and in full flow and in the next second your dead and you have flashed out of existence before your body has hit the ground.

CHAPTER 25:

It's best not to think dark thoughts at a good session in a republican house with music and the craic and a few women and of course gallons of alcohol was enough to lift anyone's spirits. I remember being at a select party were all the party goers were Republican sympathisers and I felt secure enough to relax but not long after I arrived people started to make excuses to leave until there were only a hand full left I asked one of the girls what was going on and she looked embarrassed and said it's you everybody is afraid to be seen with you and they don't want to get caught up in a gun battle if the Brits try to take you everybody knows you're a Red Card and can be shot on sight. I got sick of this and people avoiding me on the street, walking the other way when they see you and hopping from foot to foot when they had to talk to you impatient to be off. On occasion I would throw caution to the winds and with one of the girls and maybe another couple I would go to the Pound Jazz Club or some of the venues around town that let in a mixed crowd and opened late and the Brits never raided. The only problem there was there would be off duty cops and orange men in the the club as well as Catholics and you ran a risk of someone seeing you who knew you. Of course the other problem was getting home and You had two choices to take your girl and walk over to the Markets to a safe house but you always stood a chance of running into a Foot Patrol on your way there or to book into a Small Hotel or B&Band stay the night this had obvious advantages as you can imagine but not all the girls wanted to sleep with you so you couldn't always do this.

The Whitefort was my pub of choice when I could get there it had a nice little bar at the front and a big lounge at the back from which there were two back doors that led into a big walled yard and the wall was just high enough to vault over in case of trouble and you were as fit as fuck. So on a cold Saturday Night myself and one of the girls got our glad rags on and ordered a taxi to take us to the pub. There was a Diddly Dee group called the Wolf Hound playing that night and I liked them as they were funny as well as being good ballad singers and there was one who played on the tin whistle a tune called the Lonesome Boatman that I particularly liked. The Pub was crowded and I knew almost all of the patrons including the two bouncers on the door who were both in the Ex-Servicemens organisation who were used by the IRA to help protect the area and to do general menial chores that the RA didn't want to do themselves. The two bouncers were personal friends of mine and they would be sure to keep an eye out for Brits and wire me off if in the case of any potential problems. As the night wore on I was really starting to enjoy myself and was getting a bit the worse for wear from too many pints. I wanted to dance with girl who was accompanying me but I found that the Revolver I was carrying a Colt .45 with a four inch barrel was too heavy for my high waist'd Flared trousers and was pulling them down at the front and threatening to fall out on the dance floor so I got my girl to take the gun and quietly slip it into her handbag , this was better and I was able to Elvis myself around the dance floor with much better style. After about five minutes of this I went to the bar and ordered a drink a pint of Bass for me and a Gin and Tonic for my bird and while he was getting the drinks for me I went to the Gents for a pee. I had no sooner started peeing than I heard the outside corridor to the Gents open and then total silence. I was the only one in the gents and felt an oh! Shit sensation in my back, I zipped up my fly and went to turn around when the toilet door burst open and a man in his thirties hurtled into the toilet and opened fire on me hitting me right through the back of my right shoulder. I bounced off the wall at the urinals and let the force throw me back toward him I was turning to face him coming around a second bullet hit me dead centre in the chest, I saw that it was a Colt .45 Auto he was using which accounted for the feeling that I was being hit with a fuckin sledge hammer. I kept up the momentum until he was close enough to come to grips with. He then did something incomprehensibly stupid he stopped shooting and looked at me obviously to see the results of his handiwork this gave me a glimmer of hope because I was now able to reach him. I had been into Judo all my life and was a 2nd Black belt and once I got a grip of him I had a chance I took him in a Hari Goshi and slammed him down on the floor tiles and before he could react and fell onto his chest with all my weight and with my head butted him in the face and heard his nose break, I wiped my forehead across his eyes to blind him or at least to get blood into his eyes and blur his vision. He tried to force the gun point at me but I grabbed the barrel and held on for dear life he then pulled the trigger and fired the gun three or four times and the cover racked forward and back slicing the palm of my hand but I still held on, he was trying to turn me over so that he could get on top of me so I stuck my face against his and bit his nose off. He made a gurgling sound and fired the pistol again trying to get a bullet into me and the gun cocked back empty, I pounded his face with my forehead again and again and he let go the gun I pushed in the Breech and Body lock and the slide slammed forward I was then left holding the gun by the barrel and used it as a hammer to pound his head to pulp. I was bleeding to death and I believed that I was going to die. I looked to my right and blood was pumping out of my neck in conjunction with my heart beats. Just when you think it's all over it isn't. I saw the door open again and a head peeped around and looked at the carnage on the floor I raised the empty gun and pointed it at him and he fired a quick shot at me and disappeared. I tried to get up and slipped on the blood on the floor but eventually pulled myself up with the aid of the sink. I looked at myself in the mirror and I looked as rough as a bear's arse all I could think of was to get my girl get my gun off her and try to get out while I still had strength. I walked out of the toilets and saw my girl across the room, I started to walk toward her and she seemed to get further away, it was like looking down a tunnel except as I passed tables full of people the women started to scream I then remember falling backward for eternity until my back hit the floor and I saw people looking down at me. I tried to tell them I had to get out of there but some of them pointed out that I would bleed to death if I didn't get to hospital immediately I said quietly and as forcefully as I could that it was my decision and I wanted to go to a hospital in the Republic and I told them that one had got away and I needed to get out, there and then if I was to have any chance at all. One of the bouncers took off his shirt and screwed it into the hole in my back and chest and taped it up quickly as they rushed me to a fish van that had a freezer unit on top of it and shoved me in. My last conscious thought was what am I going to do with the .45 Revolver my girlfriend had shoved in to my waistband just before the van pulled away. There was only the driver my bird and myself in the van and the driver was panicking , he didn't know his way to Dundalk, what happens if we get stopped they'll kill the three of us . I called my bird close to me and said to her this guy is a wanker he's going to get us killed, listen go to this address its Clingers billet and get him to get his weapons and take over the driving this asshole is going to get me killed dump him out and tell him to keep his mouth shut or somebody will shut it for him. Clinger was right on my wave length he jumped into the van right away and told the driver to go straight home and stay there and if Clinger ever heard anything to the contrary he would come for him and kill his whole fuckin family. Then he gunned the engine and we took off I told him to check the van was full of Diesel and he said listen Boss im in charge now you just lie back on that nice cold floor and concentrate on staying alive oh oh oh staying alive. I was drifting in and out of consciousness and a couple of times woke up to find Clinger in the back of the van pounding my chest "nearly lost you there chief" but if you die on me now I'll fuck you into a ditch cover you with muck and dog shite and leave you to rot "I said when I get better I'm going to kick your arse you little cunt."Such bad language for somebody who's going to hell in a basket shortly. Shut up the two of you my bird said and keep your energy for being alive when and if you reach the hospital . Clinger reckoned that the best way across the border was to stay on the main border road and take your chance at the border crossing. The road was very busy it was 1/00am and the Brits were up to their necks in traffic and they were letting a lot of cars through at a time and letting the Irish Army check a good lot of them. The Brits waved us on but the Irish Army stopped us and saw the state of the back of the van and the state of me and they called an NCO to decide what was to be done and who in all that's holy was Johnny on the spot but my old pal in the Irish Army. He cleared the way for us and a straight run through to Drogheda . The van pulled up outside the hospital and my bird gave the medical staff on duty a quick once over on what had happened to me and said their Goodbyes and left in the van before the cops arrived. The very last memory I have of that night is lying on a trolley passing under white lights that went zoom zoom zoom and a wee nurse holding my hand and a priest saying an act of contrition into my ear and I said to him come closer and I whispered into his ear "Look Father I can see our house from here."That was the last smart assed comment I made for a while because three days later when I woke up I was in so much pain that I couldn't talk never mind crack jokes. My parents and sister and my wee brother came to see me and I'm afraid I wasn't very good company. I refused to use a bed bottle and struggled in and out to the little toilet at the end of the ward it might well have been at the end of the world for the, amount of time I took getting to and fro from it, but I was convinced that the struggle would do me a power of good in terms exercising my severely weakened body. I was looking forward to seeing the consultant as I believed that I was progressing well and I kept moving in the right direction I would get out sooner rather than later the consultant came and went and never even cast an eye in my direction never mind said anything to me. I got second hand information off one of the wee nurses on the ward that they were considering cutting off my right arm and when I questioned her on it she said it was true but that no decision had been made as yet on it one way or another. She swore to me that she would keep me constantly updated and she was a staunch Republican with a brother in the Kesh. On the other side of the coin was my Special Branch guard who sat at the door of the Ward and stunk everyone out with his pipe I hoped that he would get cancer of the head and die roaring the oul bollox. He checked me every morning to ensure I was alive even though I was eating my breakfast "Well and how are youse today Johnny Ringo" Fuck off I said to which he replied "Don't worry you'll be Chuck Connors shortly the one armed Rifle man".   When he found out that my arm was on the road to recovery he was so enraged that he threw his pipe out the window I shouted over to him that's the best place for it you won't be needing a pipe were you're going. He ran at me shouting you murderous little fucker and pulled his gun waving it around the ward, he went off that evening and another Branch Man Replaced him. This one was quiet and professional and sat there watching everything. Although in a weird sense I was a bit nervy that the SAS would try for me in the hospital and the protection would do little more than slow them down. The young guard would be as useful as tits on a bull if he got in their way. Any way I was s told that I was now well enough to be sent to St Brickens Army hospital in the Pheonix Park and I didn't have to worry about the Brits anymore. There were a good few Irish Soldiers in Brickens with one ailment or another and I got to know them pretty well. They were mostly kids with bad health and worse teeth who joined the Army because it was a reliable job and the wages were ok for the times. Something similar to the Brits except the Irish army were on our side, well in actual fact they didn't know whose side they were on and cared less and some of them had lived in the same small villages all their lives. I wasn't sure how long I would be recovering but I was better than I was letting on and my arm which was my greatest worry seemed to be progressing rightly. The only fly in the ointment was the fact that I was officially informed that I wasen't to make an escape attempt as Sinn Fein was going to make a case about extradition in the High Court and If needs be In the Supreme Court. I was happy and unhappy at the same time unhappy that I had lost my chance to escape and happy because if we won the Republic of Ireland would be a safe haven for republicans ever after. So I was released on Bail and I was given a little bedsit and warned that I was to stay out of any trouble. I found this particularly hard as the Bedsit was a kip I was being given little money all my cooking tasted like shit and I was bored to tears this was nearly as bad as being in gaol However I eventually found an outlet for my particular skills in the Republic and I can't discuss them although they would have made good reading if I could have commented on things that I never did. One Christmas Eve myself and a buddy called Nam were arsing about in Moore St looking to buy the Mass Turkey but there was nothing we could get for the few bob we had left after stocking up with alcohol which obviously was our priority so we took a walk in the pissing rain up to Grafton Street to see if there was anything to be had there but like old Mother Hubbard's Cupboard it was bare or at least bare for the couple of Bob we had left. Then Nam said our favourite words "I have A cunning " plan and I waited in Stephens green for nearly an hour when I saw him come ambling along wishing everyone A happy XMass. Jesus Christ I said what the fuck have you got in the bag". Why my good man it be the Christmas Mass Fare", enough of the Ebenezer Scrooge Nam what the fuck is in there and to my surprise he turned the sack upside down and to my shock and awe out rolled a half dozen loaves of stale bread and like Jack with the magic beans He stood smiling and said proudly here we go. He made a dive for a large rock and I said here it comes and he came up with two rocks one of which he gave to me and said Come-on do you expect the Fuckin Geese to club themselves to death lets hurry up we've got a long long way for to go and we don't want the Geese eating up the bread for the stuffing, because they seem to be getting a bit rowdy. "I have a cunning plan this time I said to Nam and I stopped at the big swing front doors at front Bewleys and putting their necks in the Roller door we slammed the doors on them which killed them there wasn't a peep out of them after that The oul one who lived in the block of Bedsits asked us what we were having and we showed them the two fresh Geese and they offered to cook them for Xmass dinner if we supplied the Geese and half of the drink. We struck a deal then and there.

CHAPTER 26:

It was the and best Xmass dinner we ever had There was only one thing which slightly bothered me was that on Boxing day I awoke in her room naked and with my mickey sore and she never said a word just sat beside me all the time and constantly rubbed me all over, we were moving on after that and she said I was a hero and although she was about fifty she looked good for her age and I took her to bed and rode her for the whole afternoon the day before I left. I sometimes .wondered what happened to her after that. It was one of those unfortunate things that the Republican Movement had as a terrible black mark against it and had as a majorly negative effect on personal relationships.

Meanwhile back in lying and cheating politics the word came through that another two lads had been lifted and were going up for extradition on the same day as me it looked as though the three of us were about to take a long walk down a short plank but we had given our word and we stuck it out to the end when were found guilty for the crimes specified and were to be handed over to the RUC immediately , but we had one more chance and that was an appeal to the Supreme Court which to shorten matters found in our Favour and set us free. There was a very large crowd outside the Green St Court House and there was a rumour that we were going to be arrested by the Special Branch immediately after our release and we were to be taken to the border and handed over to the RUC .The three of us agreed that we would have a fast car standing by and a girl I knew in the crowd was to slip me a pistol as we emerged from the Court House. As we appeared a big cheer went up and the crowd surged forward and I ducked down in the crowd and pulled on a Combat Jacket and a Balaclava the three of us made a bolt for the car but the Irish Special Branch tried to block our way , well if the fuckers expected me to hesitate to use the fire arm they were gravely mistaken as I opened fire without waiting to be told by anyone and I drove the car through the Garda checkpoint at nearly a hundred miles an hour until we were clear of the crowd and heading for safety one of the lads had organised on a small farmstead belonging to his aunt when we were safe and sound in the supporters farmhouse asked me If I wanted to see the news to see if anybody had been killed or injured in the fracas I told them that they had fired first and nearly took my head off so my reply was "who gives a fuck".

I went up to bed and fell into a dreamless sleep and I slept must have the clock round and I got up to a Breakfast in peace and quiet and then go for a long walk to clear my head. The Farmstead had a very large quarry and it was alive with rabbit's .So we sat about and killed over fifty rabbits in just about an hour. Well we had Rabbit Pie, Rabbit Stew, Rabbit Casserole and Rabbit Curry. The food was only great and there was loads of it.MY name was mud now and everybody from one end of Ireland to the other knew it. We were the most feared men In Ireland volunteers on the run and we gave England her answer from the barrels of our guns. So with nothing to lose we returned to Belfast to inflict as much damage as we could before the curtain went down on the Matinee Crew.

And it was time to die dog or Shite the Licence.

GLOSSARY

Ferrets   2 Man Armored Car

Saracen   Troop Transporter

Pig   Prisoner /Troop Transporter

Run Back   Escape Route

Stickies   Member Official IRA

VC   Victoria Cross

ASU   Active Service Unit

MRF   Military Reaction Force

SAS   Special Air Services

UDR   Ulster Defence Regiment

Provo   Member Provisional IRA

BA ,Brits, Japs   British Army

Exies   Republic Estate Policing Squad

PD   Prisoners Dependants Club

C Q B   Close Quarter Battle

P Check   On the street Identification

Zero   Full time Intelligence Officer

Contact   Met the enemy in Battle

Printed in Great Britain
by Amazon

38990497R00096